THE DOCTOR'S FORMER FIANCÉE

BY
CARO CARSON

Published in Great Britain 2014
by Mills & Boon, an imprint of Harlequin (UK) Limited,
Eton House, 18-24 Paradise Road, Richmond, Surrey, TW9 1SR

© 2014 Caro Carson

ISBN: 978 0 263 91262 3

23-0214

Despite a no-nonsense background as a West Point graduate and US Army officer, **Caro Carson** has always treasured the happily-ever-after of a good romance novel. After reading romances no matter where in the world the army sent her, Caro began a career in the pharmaceutical industry. Little did she know the years she spent discussing science with physicians would provide excellent story material for her new career as a romance author. Now, Caro is delighted to be living her own happily-ever-after with her husband and two children in the great state of Florida, a location which has saved the coaster-loving, theme-park fanatic a fortune on plane tickets.

For my mother, Kay Clark,
who fed me books along with my veggies

Chapter One

It was the part of his job Braden MacDowell hated most. Turning down requests. Telling someone their work was not going to pay off.

Killing dreams.

Braden pushed through the hospital's double doors with more force than was necessary. Nurses stared. Perhaps no one expected a stranger wearing a business suit rather than doctor's scrubs to be walking purposefully through a treatment area, but Braden knew this was a shortcut to the conference room.

Perhaps they thought he looked familiar. Braden knew he shared his brothers' physical features. Dr. Quinn MacDowell was the medical director here. Dr. Jamie MacDowell had left the battlefields of the Middle East to serve the city of Austin in this hospital's emergency department.

Braden nodded curtly at the staff as he kept walking down the corridors, the endless hospital corridors.

Perhaps they stared because the man he resembled the most strongly was his father, whose life-sized portrait hung in the lobby. He'd founded the hospital. Two of his sons healed the sick here. But Braden, the eldest, had traded in scrubs and cowboy boots for a suit and Testoni shoes. He'd taken his medical degree and left Austin for the high-stakes world of corporate America.

The staff might be wondering which MacDowell he was, but they'd know soon enough. He was the MacDowell returning home to kill someone's dream.

Braden took two flights of stairs rather than wait for the elevator. This hospital was still as familiar to him as the back of his hand. He'd practically lived here during his residency, which was how he knew this shortcut would let him avoid the hospital's chapel.

He'd face that memory later.

Not before this meeting. His emotions didn't need to be churned up before he wreaked havoc with someone else's. Braden had killed dreams before, and he'd do it again for as long as he was in the biotech industry. Eliminating this program would free up millions of dollars for more promising research. For his own sanity, he kept the end goal clearly in mind: better health for all patients, everywhere.

Scientists of all disciplines patented new theories, new molecules, new devices. However, the kind of mind that came up with potential medical solutions rarely had the business acumen to turn those ideas into reality. Millions of dollars were required to fund the years of studies that were needed to prove that an idea would actually help the average patient.

The overwhelming majority of the time, it didn't.

Then the hopeful inventor—and Braden's company—
were out millions of dollars and years of effort, and had
nothing, not one thing, to show for it.

At what point was it nearly certain that the gamble
was not going to pay off? Plaine Laboratories International relied on Braden to make that call. He was the
man expected to know when to cut PLI's losses, when
to halt the studies under way, when to give up looking
for a cure down that particular alley.

And then, on days like today, Braden got to inform everyone involved that he'd decided their dream was over.

Renovations and new wings had been added to the
hospital during his six-year absence, so at the conclusion of his shortcut, Braden had to rely on a sign to point
him down a new corridor. The old conference room had
apparently made way for an entire conference center.

Maybe the hospital chapel had been renovated or re-
located. A pang of regret hit him. Maybe he wouldn't
get the chance to say goodbye.

Impatient with himself for wasting his energy on nos-
talgia, Braden followed the signs through the new wing.
A visit to the chapel would have been only a symbolic
goodbye today. His first engagement was long over, and
Braden was ready to move on. Ready to propose to his
current girlfriend. Saying goodbye to the memory of his
former fiancée wasn't strictly necessary.

Pulling his company's funding for this project was.

The new wing made West Central feel as strange to
him as every other hospital he'd been to. He'd called on
too many hospitals to count, flying from coast to coast,
living in airports as he'd once lived in this hospital. But
PLI rewarded him, raising his pay often and substan-
tially, to keep him from being tempted by rival companies who tried to lure him away. There weren't many

executives who held both an M.D. and a Harvard MBA, so Braden was on the radar as a potential executive for practically every global biotech corporation.

As president of research and development for PLI, Braden flew less often now. He allowed his handpicked regional directors to screen the applications and research sites. He let them build the thick skin they needed to cut failing programs.

Braden personally flew in when the stakes were at their highest. Only the biggest investment. Only the biggest potential for return. Now his career had brought him full circle, back to where he'd started. Back to Texas.

Today, he'd kill a dream at the hospital where his own most valuable, most precious dream had died.

Dr. Lana Donnoli had been given less than an hour's notice for this meeting. Her predecessor, the esteemed Dr. Montgomery, had once been the faculty adviser during her residency in this hospital. He'd survived a myocardial infarct weeks ago, a common heart attack that must have caused him to reconsider his career. From his hospital bed, he'd called her office at the Washington, D.C., hospital where she worked and had offered her his position. It was an opportunity she couldn't refuse, a chance to skip a few rungs to get higher on her career ladder. For that, she could face Texas again.

She'd given her two-week notice, packed up her apartment's meager contents in a do-it-yourself moving van and driven from the mushy snow on the gray Potomac River to the cool and dry hill country of brown Central Texas. Dr. Montgomery had welcomed her with a brief handshake, announced that he was leaving before the job gave him another heart attack and literally walked out the door.

This morning. Monday. Her first day as the new chair of the Department of Research and Clinical Studies at West Central Texas Hospital had started with a bang.

West Central. It was a fine hospital with a crazy name. *Is it west or is it central? You're either in the west or in the center; you can't be both.* Every time she saw the hospital's name on a sign, she heard the lightly mocking question in her mind. The voice that posed the question was always the same: always masculine, always affectionate. Always her ex-fiancé's.

It had been a running joke between them, becoming so ingrained in her psyche that the thought played automatically, even six years after he'd left his medical training behind and moved to Boston. Six years after he'd traded in his white coat and stethoscope for an MBA from the prestigious Harvard University. Six years after he'd left her, his supposedly beloved fiancée, behind. Alone.

Still, she could hear his laughter: *Is it west or is it central?*

She pushed open the double doors with more force than necessary. The nurses stared, perhaps surprised at the amount of force coming from someone as petite as she was. Her Italian-American grandfather had fallen in love with her Polynesian grandmother in the South Pacific during World War II. Lana could have inherited her very black hair from either grandparent, but her grandmother's genes had given her hair its straightness and her eyes just a touch of an almond shape—and the petite height that came with both Polynesian traits.

If I can be an Italian-Pacific-Asian-American, why can't the hospital be West Central? Are you saying I'm an oxymoron?

No, you're a perfect combination. Hands down the sexiest, brainiest, beautiful-est—

Beautiful-est?

Beautiful-est, unique-est woman on earth, and I'm smart enough to make you mine.

Braden had tapped the diamond she'd worn on her finger, the proof of his undying love.

He'd given her the ring in the middle of their third year of medical school. On their way to the surgical suite where they'd been interning, he'd taken her by the hand and pulled her into the quiet, dim light of the hospital's small chapel, gotten down on bended knee and popped the question. She'd floated through their shift that day— her ring tucked into her bra so it wouldn't poke through her latex gloves—feeling happy even when her arms had ached from holding retractors for hours while a thoracic surgeon repaired someone else's damaged heart.

For the next year, just a glance at the ring had made her feel good, even when she was on the eighteenth hour of her day, walking down these same corridors to yet another patient.

With an impatient smack of her file against her thigh, Lana stopped her memories. She'd known coming back here would trigger them, not that they'd ever completely stopped. But she'd long ago acknowledged that the past was the past, and it shouldn't prevent her from taking advantage of this new position. The desire to avoid memories of her former fiancé wouldn't prevent her from grabbing the best opportunity she—or anyone in her field—could hope for. It was a great step toward her future, as the single but successful Dr. Lana Donnoli, a woman on the cutting edge of research, bringing new cures and new hope to patients across the country.

There was nothing wrong with being single. There was nothing wrong with being successful.

Wasn't that what you told Braden when you broke your engagement, that you understood his dedication to his career?

She was using this corridor only as a shortcut to the conference room, not to circumvent the hospital chapel.

The conference room was dead ahead. Money for the hospital—for *her* hospital—was at stake, but she knew very little about this research project. If the study was failing to show results, it could be canceled. They'd lose over a million in funding. That much, she'd been able to learn in the hour since her administrative assistant had told her this meeting was on her morning's schedule.

She was going to have to think fast to keep up with the representative from Plaine Labs International who'd come to hear the status of the study being conducted at West Central.

Is it west or is it central? You can't be both.

She wouldn't have time for memories.

Thank God.

Chapter Two

Braden tapped his fingers impatiently on the conference room's table while a senior resident fumbled with the projector for her laptop. She'd told him three times that Dr. Montgomery, Braden's former faculty adviser, had asked her to present the study's midpoint data.

When the laptop's screen was finally, successfully projected on the wall, Braden took advantage of that awkward moment before the young doctor clicked on the icon that would start the slide show. He'd become an expert at gathering all kinds of intelligence in those seconds. File names that looked personal indicated that any PLI-provided laptops were not being used strictly for research. The name of any file often indicated how many versions existed. Always, Braden would note the amount of total slides before the first one ballooned up to fill the full screen—in this case, slide one of forty-three.

Forty-three.

Death by PowerPoint. It looked as though this resident planned to make it a slow, painful death.

Braden would cut it short after a polite amount of slides had passed. He'd already received the raw data from the midpoint of this study. He'd done the statistical analysis himself. While there was some trend toward the treatment group having a better outcome than the placebo group, there was no statistical difference. Plaine Labs International was not going to sink another 1.2 million dollars and another eighteen months of time into this study, not with such weak results at the midpoint.

It was a shame, because Braden had a soft spot in his heart for the subject: a new medicine for migraines, something his father had suffered from. The man had been a force to be reckoned with, but Braden had been awed as a child at seeing his indefatigable father laid low within moments of a migraine's onset. This particular molecule wasn't going to work, though. It was time for PLI to cut its losses and move on.

Time to kill someone's dream.

The door behind him opened with a hard push, and the PowerPoint physician looked up from her laptop and exhaled in relief. "Ah, Dr. Donnoli is here—our new department chair. She'll be able to field any questions after the presentation, I'm sure."

Dr. Donnoli? Dr. Donnoli was in West Central Texas Hospital? It couldn't be. She was in Washington, D.C., adding more impressive credentials to her curriculum vitae. He knew, because he knew where all the key research physicians in America were. But he swiveled his chair to look, and it was her.

The beautiful-est girl in the world.

Damn it all to hell.

* * *

Lana crossed the beige carpet to the conference table, taking care to walk as if she were as confident as she hoped she looked in her high heels and her dark blue coat dress.

"Dr. Donnoli?" A young woman in a lab coat addressed her. "Would you like to make the presentation to Mr. MacDowell?"

MacDowell? Lana's gaze darted from the woman to the man in the dark suit. He'd been sitting with his back to the door when she'd walked in, but now he was facing her. Braden MacDowell. *Her* Braden MacDowell.

For a moment, she was frozen. Confused. It was as if being in this hospital had not only refreshed all her memories, but actually conjured her ex-fiancé in the flesh. Quite a magic trick—an unwelcome, unwanted trick of the mind.

Her administrative assistant, a compact ball of energy one would hesitate to label "elderly," burst through the door behind her.

"Sorry I'm late," the gray-haired Myrna said. "Oh, good. I see you've got that projector working."

Lana barely processed the words. Every brain cell was occupied with Braden. He looked just the same. It took only one glance for her to recall the feel of his skin, every angle of his jaw, the texture of his dark hair sliding through her fingers. Myrna kept talking as she placed notepads around the table. Lana was grateful for the valuable seconds it provided to regain her composure.

"You must be the president of Plaine Labs," Myrna was saying, making small talk and saving Lana. "Cheryl called me this morning to say you'd be here. I didn't realize you were already in the building. Welcome to our conference center. May I introduce our new chairperson,

Dr. Lana Donnoli?" She gestured at Lana. "Dr. Donnoli, this is Mr. Braden MacDowell."

Braden stood and nodded at Lana politely. Impersonally. How did he manage it? Was she nothing more than a past memory, an old college girlfriend?

"Dr. Donnoli," he said, and the bored formality in his voice went straight to her heart. And it hurt.

That he could still have that kind of power over her, six years after leaving her behind, made her angry. She extended her hand to shake his, determined to show him the professional she was, not the heartbroken girl he probably remembered sobbing over a phone line.

"*Mr.* MacDowell?" she asked, with a skeptical lift of her brow. "Isn't it Dr. MacDowell?"

"I don't use the title." He shook her hand firmly, once, and let go.

"Why not? You earned that much." She knew she'd made it sound as if it wasn't much at all.

"I'm well aware that it's an academic title only. Since I don't practice medicine, I don't choose to use it."

Myrna stopped in the middle of placing her pens. "Do you two already know each other?" She sounded a little confused, and a little hopeful.

"Not at all," Lana said tersely at the same time that Braden said, "Very well."

"Ah," Myrna said, looking confused but obviously too smart to explore that topic further. Instead, she gestured toward the senior resident, who was standing by her laptop, finger poised on the enter key. "This is Dr. Everson. She joined our department this month."

"My card," Braden said, offering Lana a small rectangle of pressed linen paper.

"Thank you." She should have offered him her card, of course, but she hadn't had a chance to get any made.

Instead, she asked the very young-looking Dr. Everson
to please begin the presentation and took a seat directly
across from Braden, on the opposite side of the nar-
row table.

As the resident began with slide number one, Lana
glanced down at the card in her hand. The initials of
the corporate giant formed the familiar PLI logo in gold
and burgundy ink. Very expensive ink, as she recalled
from the days she'd spent at stationery stores, choosing
wedding invitations. She and Braden, up to their necks
in med school student loans, hadn't been able to afford
colored engraving like this. They'd planned to send their
wedding invitations in plain, formal black ink, like his
name on this business card:

Braden MacDowell, M.D., MBA
President of Research and Development

His business card was very impressive, if one admired
money-making over life-saving. She did not. She never
had. It had crushed her when Braden had decided he did.

Lana pretended not to look at Braden as he patiently
listened to the resident explain slide number two. Braden's
tie was a subtle symphony of colors on silk. His watch
was worth as much as her worn-out car, she was certain.
But his face no longer reflected enthusiasm for life, and
his mouth no longer lifted in an easy smile. Chasing the
almighty dollar had not been a happy way for him to
spend the past six years, apparently.

Lana had made the right choice by breaking their engagement. She could not have been the right wife for this
executive. He'd been heading in that profit-driven direction then; she wasn't going to regret it now.

No—she was going to ignore him for the duration of

the PowerPoint presentation, because she needed to read every slide and learn all she could about this study. Her one goal, her only goal, was to keep PLI's funding coming into this hospital.

She slid another look at his painfully familiar profile. He was handsome, classically handsome, but her eye went to the imperfections, the ones she'd known and loved. His eyes had some crinkles at the corners, as they'd had even six years ago, from a youth spent ranching in the relentless Texas sun. His chin had a scar from being cut open too many times for him to recount them all to her. Being thrown from a horse. Getting sacked in high school football. Attempting some prank with his brother. He looked like an urbane city man now, a business tycoon in a Savile Row suit, but that scar on his chin revealed the man he'd been. Lana knew him, under that suit.

Under that suit, he was…

Warm skin and hard muscle. Every inch of him.

For God's sake, Lana. You're the department chair. Pay attention.

More than a million dollars were at stake. West Central was counting on her to achieve one simple goal: renew PLI's contract.

Perhaps she ought to set a second goal. She was going to keep her heart well guarded from the dreamy Dr. MacDowell.

"Thank you for that thorough presentation," Lana said.

She would coach Dr. Everson later about making her presentations less lengthy. In front of PLI's president, however, Lana would point out only the positive for the sake of West Central Hospital. Thankfully, the study in question had turned out to be for a medicine she'd also been studying in Washington. Lana felt a little more secure in her knowledge. "It's exciting that pentagab has met the midpoint goals."

Which meant *it's exciting that we'll be extending our contract with PLI.*

"I regret that PLI will not be continuing this study." It was the first thing Braden had said in forty minutes. Lana heard that familiar voice, still masculine, but no longer infused with affection for her. It took a moment for his words to sink in through the miasma of emotional memories.

"You're not continuing this study?" she asked. "But this drug shows such promise."

"I don't believe it does."

"But the numbers—let's go back to that last graph—"

"The graph looks impressive, yes, but it's just drawn cleverly. The raw numbers make the treated group appear to be doing better than the placebo group, but where is the p-value? There is no statistical significance."

Startled, Lana looked at the screen. The bar graph looked straightforward, but sure enough, the standard line that stated the p-value between the groups was missing. The p-value was a mathematical calculation used to determine if the difference between two groups mattered. If one hundred patients responded to a medicine but ninety patients responded to a placebo, that ten-patient difference was not really a difference. Not in the world of science.

"The statistical analysis was on another slide," she said, stalling for time. It was on one of forty-three slides. Lana flipped through her paper copies of the PowerPoint presentation, doing some frantic speed-reading. "Here it is," she said with relief. "P equals point-zero-five. Statistically significant, and it looks like the data are trending toward a more robust end point."

Still, she'd have to ask Everson why the p-values hadn't been clearly listed on the graph itself, where they typically were in medical studies.

"Those numbers are wrong," Braden said in a tone as certain as if he'd said *the sky is blue*.

"How can you say that off the top of your head?"

Braden only raised an eyebrow.

Of course, he knew that she knew he was a math whiz. He probably could look at a bar graph and come up with a p-value without touching a calculator, let alone performing a page of equations.

"Never mind." Lana turned to Dr. Everson, who was looking younger and less reliable by the minute. "Who prepared these slides? Who ran our numbers?"

"Uh, well, I was instructed to do some preliminary work, and then Dr. Montgomery finalized it."

Dr. Montgomery, who couldn't stay one more hour to take this meeting. Lana had a sinking feeling. Had Dr. Montgomery been so desperate to keep this funding that he'd do something unethical? Surely not. This had to be an honest mathematical error. An error that just happened to be in their favor.

One that, had it gone unchallenged, would have kept more than one million dollars coming into the hospital.

How badly in debt was her department? How hard would the cancellation of this study hit them? Her?

She was determined not to find out; she was going to save this study.

"Myrna, Dr. Everson. If the two of you could excuse us, I'd like to take the rest of this meeting one-on-one with Dr. MacDowell."

Chapter Three

Lana had never groveled to Braden, not even when she'd so desperately wanted him to stay in Texas instead of moving across the country to Boston. Now she groveled. Begged.

"Please, give me a day to run these numbers again. I just left Washington, where I was involved in the sister study to this one, the pediatric study. Our results were clearly significant. If the pediatric results were good, then odds are that the adult results are as well, so if you'll just give me time to calculate—"

"I ran the numbers myself, Lana, before I came here. Personally."

An old, defensive feeling resurfaced. "Because you knew I'd be here? It's been years since I needed your help to pass statistics class. I know how to interpret data."

He cut her off before her indignation could build more

steam. "I always run the numbers myself before committing millions of research dollars."

She couldn't stay impersonal; the memories were just too bitter. "I should have known it would come down to making a profit for you."

His expression stayed impassive, but she caught the movement of muscle as he clenched his jaw.

Don't bite the hand that feeds you—or feeds West Central Hospital.

Lana buried her personal feelings. "I was running that pediatric study in D.C. To be studying migraines in pediatrics was rare enough, but even more unusual, the results were positive. Please, Braden, I'm pleading for a second chance here. Let the second half of the study go forward."

"There's no gain in—"

"We'll gain knowledge. Practically every study has shown that adult migraine medicines work poorly in children. This could be the exception to the rule. Even if the adult trial fails, the significance of a drug working for pediatrics but not adults will be novel and worthy of further research."

She could recall the individual faces of children enrolled in the Washington study. How miserable they were, in pain. How much happier they were when the drug started working. As their pain receded, their personalities emerged, happy kids who made her laugh. She couldn't let them down. Losing the adult study here at West Central would hurt her professionally, but keeping the pediatric one funded was personal. Those children, her patients, mattered. Not profits.

"Even if the results are novel, who is going to fund that further research, Lana? PLI isn't going to."

"Why not?" She wanted to pound the table in frustration. "I'm telling you, the data in peds is rock-solid."

"Because there's no money in treating pediatric migraines."

No money in it?

She'd told herself a hundred times that the man she'd once loved cared only about profits. That he'd chosen not to practice medicine with her because he'd wanted the bigger dollars offered in the business world. She'd clung to that as her justification for ending their engagement.

Always, he'd protested that money wasn't his motive for going to Harvard Business School instead of staying with her at West Central. He'd denied that the need to excel in the corporate world was the reason he no longer wanted to open a husband-and-wife family practice in Texas. Some part of her must have believed him after all, because now, to hear him say it himself—*there's no money in treating pediatric migraines*—was devastating.

Even after six years.

Braden watched the light in Lana's eyes die, the passion in her expression fade. It was the same look he'd seen on the faces of other hopefuls whose dreams he'd had to kill. The fact that it was Lana this time didn't make it any different.

Braden felt very tired. Too old, too wise to the ways of the world.

"This is the reality of the marketplace," he said. "Pediatric migraineurs are only a fraction of all patients."

"You saw these slides. They estimate over twenty-nine million Americans suffer from migraines. Even if only a few percent are pediatric, that's still a million or more patients. That's huge."

"No, it's not. Only half of your twenty-nine million

even know their headaches are migraines to begin with. Only half of *those* will seek help from a physician, and less than half of those might be prescribed a drug like this one. Another percentage will never fill the prescription. There are barely enough adult sufferers to make a new migraine drug viable. There are not enough children."

"To make the medicine viable? You mean profitable."

"I mean viable. Can it begin to recoup the millions—the hundreds of millions—that were spent on bringing it to the local drugstore? I estimate that only one in five drugs that makes it to the public sells enough pills to cover the cost of inventing it in the first place."

"I'm talking patients here. There may not be a lot of them, but there are children out there who suffer terribly from migraines. They're in pain, Braden. They can't play and go to school. What about them?"

At the moment, Braden hated his job with a passion. Why did he have to be the one destroying Lana's dreams? Let someone else disillusion her.

She kept championing her cause. "The adult medicines don't work well to relieve the pain for children. Most of the treatments aren't even FDA approved for pediatric use—"

"As it should be. They don't work well in pediatrics. Lana, step back and look at the big picture. When the first one or two migraine medicines ran pediatric studies, they failed. They didn't work. Why should the other drugs in the same class throw time and money down the same drain?"

"Money. Always money. What about the patients?"

"I *am* thinking about patients. There is only so much money out there. What should we spend it on? Who needs it most?" He'd heard her words a dozen times before.

She'd always maintained that if he cared about people, he'd be a physician, not a corporate executive.

He felt himself sucked into a time warp of sorts. Felt himself once more losing the woman he loved as she accused him of placing money before all else.

As he had a dozen times before, he tried to make her understand. "This is what I do, Lana. These are the life-and-death decisions I make now. Should I fund a pediatric migraine study that might—and I emphasize might—improve the quality of life for a fraction of a percent of all children? Or should I take those same funds—because by God, there are only so many dollars out there—should I take those same funds and invest them to develop a cardiac medicine that could prevent millions of deaths?"

He was standing, he realized, as was she. They were glaring into each other's eyes, battling for supremacy. Again. Always.

"You make that call, Lana. Should I help three million kids who have episodes of pain, or should I help eighty million adults, the parents and grandparents of those children, who are facing death? You choose, because I don't have enough money to do both."

She stayed silent, but she didn't back down, not in her body language, and not in her glare. Why had he thought this time would be different?

Braden berated himself for letting her bait him into this debate. None of it mattered. Their entire conversation wasn't going to change the fact that PLI was withdrawing further funding. He wasn't going to throw more money at an unlikely solution to what amounted to a rare problem in the universe of medical crises.

And Lana was not going to understand him now any more than she'd understood him then. He'd had six years to stop wanting her to understand him. Wanting her to respect his career. Wanting her to trust him, to support him.

Wanting her.

She was so damned vibrant, so passionate, so beautiful. The temptation to end this match with a crushing kiss was overwhelming. That physical attraction had become a crutch for them, toward the end. They couldn't agree on their careers and their future, so they'd fall into bed and have silent, soul-searing sex.

In Lana's opinion, they'd had sex one time too many. The last time had had consequences neither of them had been ready for.

Still, he found himself craving the smoothness of her skin, the curves of her body, the surrender of herself. Six years hadn't been long enough apart. He needed another six to kill his desire for Lana Donnoli—and he wasn't going to spend it waiting for absolution and understanding in this conference room.

"I regret to inform you that Plaine Laboratories International has decided to end all trials of NDA zero two one zero six one. West Central's contract will expire in accordance with our prior arrangements, and no renewals will be pursued. Goodbye, Dr. Donnoli."

Braden's decision was final. Lana knew it; she watched him close his laptop case with a single click of a lock.

He's leaving, and I failed.

The expression on his face was no longer fierce, no longer focused on her. He looked withdrawn. Remote. He was already gone, although he was still in the room with her. Then he picked up his briefcase and was gone for real. The door closed after him with a firm, controlled click.

I failed him.

Him? Not only the hospital, but him?

Somehow, he'd been disappointed in her, yet Braden had no right to expect anything from her. What had he wanted?

Professionally, her failure was simple to define. She'd failed to keep this hospital's study going. Failed in her new responsibility to get financing for the research branch of West Central Texas Hospital.

Is it west or is it central? You can't have both.

She couldn't have the migraine trials, but could she have something else instead? They had the facilities. They had the staff, the patient flow—there must be other studies that PLI needed a site like West Central for. There were other funds she could secure for her department.

She stopped debating with herself and started walking after Braden. Quickly. She needed to talk to him today, before he walked out of the hospital completely, like he'd once walked out of her life.

Breathless from catching up to his much longer strides, she followed him to the bank of elevators. The doors started to slide open before she could reach him.

"Braden, don't go!"

The back of his head jerked up, just a bit. He turned her way and stood still, not moving away from the elevator, but not stepping into the car, either. She was suddenly so afraid he might leave without her, she jogged the last few steps to him and put her hand on his sleeve.

"Don't go yet. Please."

He placed his warm hand over hers. There was a clear question in his eyes, a concerned tilt of his head, a softening of the hard mask of his face. "Why not, Lana?"

"I want a second chance. I want to talk to you about PLI."

He removed his hand to stab the button to recall the elevator. "The decision is made. I can't explain it any better. If you don't understand, that's your problem."

"No—no, that's just it. I do understand. PLI only has a limited amount of research dollars to go around. But I want a second chance."

The elevator doors opened and Braden walked into the waiting car, away from her. She followed, grateful that the car was empty.

"Listen, Braden, please. I just got into town. Dr. Montgomery walked out, literally, minutes after I arrived this morning. I haven't had a chance to get my bearings or take stock of what we have here, but I know West Central has a lot to offer in the way of research facilities and staff, far more than it did when we were residents here."

She made her best case while she had him trapped in the elevator. "Give me the rest of today to review my department. PLI and West Central can use each other, I'm sure of it. You must have dozens of studies under way, and there is always a need for another enrollment site."

He didn't agree or disagree. He only watched her as she pleaded.

She touched his sleeve again. "Will you give me a day? If I find out what I still have to offer you, would you be willing to consider me again?"

He let several seconds of silence tick by before he spoke. "Will I consider what you have to offer? That's one hell of a question, coming from my former fiancée."

Whatever answer she'd expected, it hadn't been that. Not that personal. They'd kept everything strictly professional to this point. It felt as though he'd violated some invisible boundary by bringing up their intimate past so bluntly.

The elevator stopped to let an elderly couple on. The

man was in a wheelchair; the woman was pushing him with the ease of long experience. He made a gesture to his right, and she picked up the paperwork that was tucked under his right side and placed it in his hand. Effortless communication.

Had anything been as easy between her and Braden? *Yes—making love.*

And they'd conceived a baby. Too easily. Without trying. Without wanting to.

She'd miscarried that pregnancy the same way.

The memory threatened to completely breach any wall she'd maintained to this point. Before it could overwhelm her, she spoke quickly and quietly to Braden.

"You know perfectly well that West Central has excellent resources to conduct research. You need facilities and patient bases and sites. Just give me a day to get my bearings, and we can meet again to find out how we can help one another's *companies.*"

The elevator reached the lobby level. Braden maintained his silence.

She didn't. "You know I need to replace the funds you just withdrew. I'll be offering West Central to other biotechs and pharmas."

She had seconds to convince him as he courteously waited for the wheelchair couple to exit. "If you don't want what I have to offer, someone else will. I'm giving you the right of first refusal."

Braden cut his gaze to her. She stayed where she was, silently demanding an answer.

He walked out of the elevator instead.

"Braden," she called after him. Damn it all, she was losing him. Losing PLI's funding.

Braden turned around and looked her up and down, just once, as she stayed in the elevator.

"I'm returning to New York. Now. The PLI representative for the state of Texas is Cheryl Gassett. I'm sure your assistant knows her and has her contact information. If you find that you can make PLI an offer, call Cheryl."

The elevator doors slid closed, separating them with finality.

Alone, Lana knew she could cry without embarrassment. She could punch the door with impunity. She could collapse in a heap of exhaustion.

None of it would change the past. She pushed the button that reopened the doors, exited the elevator and walked in the opposite direction that Braden had taken, toward her office. Toward her future.

Braden's rejection had changed the course of her life once. She couldn't let him derail her again.

Chapter Four

Braden needed to leave the hospital. He was done here. *Done.* There were too many emotions. Too many bad memories.

Too much Lana. Here, in the flesh. Not a memory of her, which he'd come ready to bury. No, the woman herself was here. Vibrant. Passionate. Real.

He was too old to be blinded by sexual attraction. Chemistry had never been their problem, so it shouldn't surprise him now that it still existed at some level.

A level a little too dammed close to the surface…

He walked past the chapel without slowing, without stopping, without so much as throwing a glance at its doors. The entire reason he'd bothered himself with flying to West Central personally had been to stop in that chapel. He'd proposed to Lana there, and he'd had some idiotic notion that by saying goodbye to the memory of that promise, he'd be free to propose to another woman, elsewhere.

God, he was a fool. What an idiotic, sappy idea for a man of science and business to entertain, let alone act upon. If he was ready for a permanent relationship, then he'd make a commitment to the woman of his choice, and damn his youthful college engagement to hell. Lana certainly had. She'd dumped him over the phone and mailed his engagement ring to his Harvard address in an empty tongue depressor box.

Six years ago. He was over it. He was dating Claudia St. James now, a woman who could make a perfect wife for a professional man like himself, but damn it, seeing Lana in person had been a shock. *Braden, don't go,* she'd practically shouted, and the plea in her voice had kept him from stepping on the elevator. His response had probably been an old reflex, a bad habit ingrained long ago. Still, it had been damned disconcerting.

He stopped abruptly at the corner of a garden fountain, disoriented for a fraction of a second. There was a fountain in the lobby now? Yes, and he'd nearly walked into it, distracted by thoughts of Lana.

He should not be distracted by his past. He'd come here to begin his future, and he'd already picked out the right woman to spend the rest of his life with. Claudia never caused him to walk into fountains, thank God.

Braden kept walking, past the paintings of his father and the other founders, not breaking his stride as he threw a glance at the modern domed ceiling. The renovated lobby looked more like it belonged to an elegant hotel than a hospital. It was a far cry from the single-story construction his father had begun. Would his father have approved of the changes if he'd lived to see them?

Braden imagined that patients who were sick and worried would appreciate the welcome this new lobby extended. It had an air of grace and authority that could be reassuring when patients arrived with serious health concerns. They'd probably feel hope, as though they'd come to the right place. His father, Braden decided, would have approved of the modern West Central. He would have approved of the job his son was doing.

That son being Quinn, of course. Quinn was the only MacDowell on the hospital board.

Dad had not approved of the job I was doing.

His father had always expected him to follow in his footsteps. Braden had tried. He'd tried for his father's sake, and then he'd kept trying after he'd met Lana, but by his last year of residency, he'd known the life of a family-practice physician was not for him.

He'd wanted to show his father and his fiancée that his life could be a different kind of success. He *had* shown them, really. He'd graduated magna cum laude from arguably the best graduate school in the country, perhaps in the world. He'd gone on to be a key player in the biotech industry, working to contribute valuable medicines and devices not just to the city of Austin but to all people, all around the globe. But his dad had died before that first patent had made it to the marketplace, before he'd been able to prescribe any of the drugs his son had chosen to develop.

And Lana? Hell, she'd mailed his ring back before he'd even graduated.

Still, Braden was one of the most successful men in America, if only someone besides his accountant appreciated it.

Claudia St. James appreciates success.

Exactly. He needed to keep his thoughts in the present. Braden realized his steps had taken him to the former main entrance of the emergency department. An involuntary smirk lifted one corner of his mouth despite his bitter feelings. Not even the resurrected emotions of a broken engagement and a disapproving father could disengage his mind completely. His day's agenda had included a quick visit to his younger brother, another physician, of course. Jamie worked here in the emergency department. Without trying, Braden had stayed on schedule.

This entrance to the E.R. was now a shortcut for staff only, and the heavy double doors were unlocked when personnel waved a badge in front of the security box on the wall. A man in scrubs stepped up to the box and lifted his name tag. A tiny light blinked from red to green, and the doors swung open slowly. The man nodded at Braden deferentially, probably assuming he was an off-duty physician.

Technically, Braden was a physician, one who was not on duty. The man had made an accurate assumption, then. Braden returned the man's nod and followed him into the treatment area. He stopped at the centrally located wraparound desk. "Where can I find Dr. MacDowell?"

The nurse he'd addressed frowned at him slightly. "And you are…?"

From long practice, he smiled at her with just the right amount of professional friendliness. "Please tell Dr. MacDowell that Dr. MacDowell is here to see him."

Her frown lifted into a smile. "I should have guessed from the resemblance. He's just back from his honeymoon, but you must be one of the bachelor MacDowells." She tilted her head at an attractive angle and winked at him.

Braden returned her smile with very little effort. The world was returning to normal. Women liked him. He liked women. It was only Lana Donnoli that made him feel irritated. Angry. Vaguely dissatisfied with his life.

"Is that you, Braden? Can't be. That would make three times in one year that you've come to Texas."

Braden turned at the sound of his brother's voice. Jamie was the youngest son, Braden the eldest. They shook hands, which quickly morphed into a one-armed hug. More of a slap on the shoulders, really. They were exactly the same height, something that never failed to catch Braden by surprise. Jamie had only been in middle school when Braden had left for college. Somehow, Braden always expected him to still be the runt baby brother.

"What's the occasion?" his six-foot-tall runt of a brother asked. "Is New York City finally wearing on you? Don't tell me you missed me."

Braden should have had a quick comeback for that one, the kind of jokingly derogatory comment brothers would exchange, but he was startled into a momentary silence by the realization that he had, in fact, missed Jamie. It had been good to see him at a charity event in the fall. Even better to see him for a few days in December, when he'd carved out some holiday time to get to know Jamie's new wife and his baby. Jamie's family.

Family. Braden hadn't spent much time with his family after turning his back on practicing medicine. He'd avoided Texas for years after his broken engagement, if he was honest with himself, but that was about to change. Whether Lana would be here or not, it was time to come back home.

Braden would soon announce that PLI was investing millions in a new research center. It had taken all the business savvy he'd gained over the years to pull it off, and he'd cashed in every chip he'd been owed, but Braden had convinced PLI's board to build the facilities in Austin. Just as his father had contributed this hospital to the community, Braden would contribute a major biotech research and development site to his hometown.

Look, Dad, I'm following in your footsteps.

The tension in his shoulders eased. Had he lived to see it, his father would have been unconditionally proud. Braden knew that. He expected his mother and brothers would feel the same way when they found out.

Braden couldn't tell them yet. The Securities and Exchange Commission had strict rules against corporate presidents leaking that kind of information too soon. For now, he'd have to content himself with giving his baby brother a hard time.

"As if your ugly mug would be enough to drag me across the country," he said, resisting the urge to throw a fake slo-mo punch at Jamie. Those childhood habits died hard. "But your wife's pretty face, that's another matter. Is Kendry working today?"

"She's home, studying for an exam. Nursing school is no cakewalk. Better her than me."

"Beautiful and smart. Driven. My kind of woman."

"She's all that and more, but since married women aren't your thing, to what do we owe the pleasure of this visit?"

"This trip was strictly business," Braden lied. He wasn't about to confess his idiotic notion of visiting the chapel to formally end the promise he'd once made. "I was expecting to meet with Dr. Montgomery."

"Montgomery? That old bastard is the reason you flew across the country? Now I am offended."

"I wouldn't have wasted the jet fuel if someone had

bothered to inform me that Montgomery was no longer the head of research."

"Until yesterday, I was basking in the sun under a co-conut tree with Kendry. Good thing your company can afford the plane ticket." To the nurse, Jamie gave orders for the patient whose cubicle he'd just left. "Nebulizer in four. Call me when the azithromycin IV is finished. I'll be in the kitchen."

Braden followed Jamie into the kitchenette that the staff used during their round-the-clock shifts.

"I could have done without the surprise," Braden said, once they were alone. He still felt off balance after seeing Lana.

"What surprise?"

"Dr. Montgomery's replacement. Lana Donnoli."

"That's your Lana? From med school?"

"You didn't know?" Braden crossed his arms over his chest and eyed his brother skeptically.

"I told you, I was on a beach. On my honeymoon."

"The decision wasn't made yesterday."

"I'm just a lowly E.R. doc. You want to get pissed off at a brother, go find Quinn. He joined the board."

Braden shook off the offer of the cup of coffee Jamie had just poured, so Jamie drank it himself, settling against the counter. "It sucks being back on my feet after spending a week in bed."

"Yeah, life's rough." Braden's sarcastic answer was automatic, but he knew his younger brother deserved every bit of happiness that came his way. While serving the country as an army physician in a war zone, Jamie had lost the first woman he'd loved. He'd come a long way since that dark period, and Braden was glad to see it. Still, he didn't want to hear about honeymoon bliss. "In all seriousness, I'm glad civilian life is treating you well."

"Don't get all mushy on me. The coffee's decent. Have some."

Braden poured a cup and sat down in a plastic chair that looked like a waiting-room reject. "Lana's too young to be the department head at a hospital this size."

Jamie had the nerve to grin. "We're still on that topic? Like I said, Quinn's on the board, not me. But I noticed this morning that her name's been added to the E.R.'s coverage list. I wondered if it was your Lana."

"She hasn't been *my* anything for years. I sure as hell hope Quinn didn't give her this position out of some misguided idea that he'd be helping out an old family friend." He drank the coffee black. No cream, no sugar to hide the true flavor.

Jamie was watching him closely. As the youngest, he'd been away at college during Braden's engagement. He probably knew very little about the whole affair.

Braden explained. "Lana's the one who called it off. Mailed the ring to me at Harvard and never spoke to me again."

"And then you walked into the boardroom today and there she was?"

Braden rejected the sympathy he heard in Jamie's tone. "That wasn't an issue. I just don't want you or Quinn thinking she's some kind of family friend who deserves special consideration."

"I don't see Quinn letting your love life influence decisions about this hospital. He treats this place like Dad did, like it's some kind of gift to the community."

Hearing Jamie voice his own earlier thought out loud was both discomforting and reassuring. As children, they'd all competed with the hospital for their father's attention, Braden supposed, although he'd always felt pride in knowing the medical complex was a MacDowell legacy.

One which he, the eldest son, had left behind. One from which he'd just pulled a million dollars of funding.

The coffee tasted like hell. Braden dumped his coffee down the sink and crushed the paper cup in his hand. "It's good that Quinn takes it seriously. A nonprofit hospital is a gift to the community."

By Valentine's Day, the PLI deal would be final, and Braden would be legally able to tell his family about the research facilities, his own contribution to the city. He looked forward to proving that he was still loyal to his hometown. The project was proof that Braden hadn't abandoned his family or his father's ideals, despite the way it may have seemed on the surface for the past six years.

Until then, what were another four or five days of misunderstanding? That subtle condemnation, that distrust, that assumption that he preferred to be a loner in the big city had started when he'd left Austin for Boston. When he'd left doctoring for big business. When he'd left Lana for—

For no one. He'd never left Lana. She'd done all the leaving.

Braden, don't go. I want a second chance.

Her words today had shaken him, although she'd been talking about a second chance with his corporation, not with him. After she'd broken their engagement, he'd heard nothing but silence. If she'd spoken those words six years ago—or five, or four—he would gladly have taken her back, to be honest. But not now.

Now Braden was moving on. This Valentine's Day, he intended to stake his claim as a MacDowell in Austin's medical community. He also intended to announce the next phase of his personal life. He anticipated introducing Claudia St. James to his family, then proposing marriage to seal the deal.

After a six-year absence, he'd have a wife and an office in Austin, just as he'd always planned, although the office wouldn't be a doctor's office, and the wife wouldn't be Lana.

He tossed his cup into the trash can. PLI and Claudia St. James would suit him just fine. Just fine.

Jamie tossed his cup in the bin, as well. "You don't have to tell me the hospital is a gift. I know it is. Quinn knows it is. It's possible that he was opposed to Lana's appointment, but the rest of the board voted for it. You'll have to ask him, since you suddenly give a damn about who chairs which department here." Jamie pushed away from the counter and looked him in the eye.

Yeah, his baby brother was all grown up.

"Think about it, Braden. Your Lana is young enough to be called in to work the E.R. when we're shorthanded. Financially, I gather from Quinn that times have been tight for the hospital."

It was Braden's turn to raise an eyebrow. Finances were his area of expertise. West Central looked prosperous on the surface, but it was possible the accounts didn't paint the same rosy picture.

"Lana's age might have been a bonus," Jamie said. "She's young enough to have the stamina to cover for docs like me, and despite her years in research, she's still considered inexperienced enough to not expect a salary like Montgomery was pulling."

"If she does his job, she should get his salary. Just because she's young doesn't mean she isn't competent." *Competent* was a lukewarm word to describe the woman Braden remembered. She'd been the sharpest person in the residency program—except for himself. They'd been in hot competition, vying for the best ratings, competing for the highest evaluations. She'd kept him on his toes. She'd been his match in more ways than he could count.

"Now she's competent and not too young after all?" Jamie laughed a little. "Quinn's not an idiot. Even if Lana is getting Montgomery's salary, the hospital gets extra coverage for the E.R. out of the deal."

Braden didn't want to stand here and discuss Lana Donnoli, not when he should be preparing his family to meet Claudia. A change of subject was in order, and as brothers went, he was being a lousy one by not asking after his new nephew. "You've got a point. So, how's Sammy?"

"Fine. Better than fine, making up for lost time now that all his surgeries are behind him. He's walking now. When you feed him, he tries to grab the spoon out of your hand to feed himself." Jamie's love and pride came through with every word. His infant son had been facing medical hurdles when he'd first arrived in the States, but Jamie and his wife had helped their son leap them all.

Braden was glad to hear it. He liked kids, and he'd always expected to be a father someday. Just because it hadn't happened with Lana didn't mean it wouldn't happen. Surely Claudia would want to have children after they married.

"I think taking care of the baby while we were on our honeymoon was more than Mom could handle," Jamie said. "Call me after you see her. I want to know if she's still fatigued. Tell me if you think she's exhibiting muscle weakness—or anything else you notice."

The worry in his brother's voice was as unmistakable as his earlier pride in his child had been. Braden was instantly worried, too. Worried, but on a schedule.

"I'm flying back to New York now. This was just a fly in, fly out."

"Nothing's a 'fly in, fly out' anymore. Not when there's a two-hour security wait before every flight."

"PLI has a few private jets. Don't give me that look. It's a business necessity, not a luxury."

Jamie whistled softly. "You flew here in a private jet just to see Dr. Montgomery? It would have been a lot more interesting if you'd come to see Lana."

"I don't waste company resources."

But he had. He'd come to say farewell to Lana. Not the real woman, of course, but the memory of her. He'd failed to execute that step, but the rest of his plan was still in place. "I was going to spend Valentine's weekend at the ranch. Do you think Mom's health is too frail?"

"You should check on her. Go back to New York tomorrow. You can sleep at my place, if Mom's not up to company. My guest room's empty."

"No, thanks. The last thing I want is to be around a couple of newlyweds cooing over each other."

"If marital bliss makes you queasy, then Quinn's got a pullout sofa."

Braden just raised an eyebrow in the way he knew made him look like their father. "I'll be at the Four Seasons."

Jamie raised an eyebrow in return. He could do the MacDowell look as well as Braden could. "The Four Seasons in New York?"

"In Austin."

"Good."

Braden left the hospital through the ambulance portico as he phoned his executive assistant. She would contact the hotel and the pilot. There was always a packed suitcase on board the plane, one which would be delivered to the Four Seasons with no inconvenience to himself. Braden mentally adjusted his schedule before his assistant could answer. He would use this unexpected layover in Austin to execute another key step in his plan.

He wanted to use an Austin jeweler to create the perfect engagement ring for Claudia. Nothing in New York had seemed appropriate. But first, he'd visit his mother to be sure her health would allow her to meet the perfect potential daughter-in-law.

Valentine's Day. He was a businessman who set goals and timelines. His life would finally move on, come Valentine's Day.

Chapter Five

Lana couldn't focus on the pink paper hearts that Myrna was sticking on the door to their office. She watched Myrna painstakingly frame the square window that made up most of the top half of the door. Hopefully, a ten-second break from her computer screen was all Lana's eyes needed.

It didn't work. When she looked back at the monitor, the numbers quickly began jumping on the screen once more. They blurred before her tired eyes. Maybe she needed reading glasses. Maybe Dr. Montgomery had left an old pair behind.

Her hand reached for the desk drawer even as her eyes filled with tears. The thought of needing reading glasses made her cry, even if Braden MacDowell didn't.

"Am I that old?"

Lord, she felt it. Old and tired. It was a natural conse-quence, she was certain, from running for too many days on too little sleep. Packing up in D.C., driving halfway across the country and taking over a department in disarray left no time for rest. Of course she couldn't focus. She was tired. Not old and tired. Just tired.

But she needed to focus on these numbers. She needed to win another research contract with PLI. Braden MacDowell's company.

Braden. He was why she felt so old. Six years had passed, but they felt like sixty. Seeing Braden had been a shock, but it was already over, and Lana would be dealing with Cheryl Gassett from now on. Myrna already knew the PLI representative, in fact. It was quite possible that Lana might never see Braden again.

The thought almost made her sad. Braden was part of her lost youth.

Lost youth? She was only thirty-four. This pity party had to stop. She had a job to do.

Lana crammed her feet back into the pumps she'd kicked off. She sat up straighter in her chair and tugged her dress into place.

My completely unsexy, strictly business dress.

What had Braden thought of her severe appearance? Had he wondered what had happened to his former bed partner? Had he thanked his lucky stars that he hadn't been saddled with her as a wife after all?

God, she felt old.

She turned away from the monitor and flipped open the three-ring binder that held the paperwork for the patients in the migraine study. They'd have to be contacted, asked to return early, and their remaining pills—whether active or placebo dummies—would have to be retrieved. Lana ran her finger down the page of names. Instead of numbers, letters jumped and swam on the page. So many people, so little hope for them. How could Braden be so heartless?

He hadn't always been. She'd been engaged to a man who'd been gentle with the patients in this hospital, gentle with the horses on his ranch, gentle with her when the grueling process of becoming a doctor consumed her life. Then he'd left her and their dream of working together behind, and she'd been heartbroken that her fiancé had been driven by the need to make money.

There was no money in treating migraines, he'd said. Lana trailed her finger down the page, seeing patient after patient who would not be helped because they couldn't generate a profit.

One name, one name in the entire bunch, jumped off the page, crystal clear, in perfect focus.

Oh, Braden, how could you?

His own mother was about to lose her chance for pain relief. Marion MacDowell had been receiving the active medicine.

Lana glanced at Braden's card. She'd set it off to the side of her desk. Lana was not supposed to deal with PLI's president directly, but this Cheryl Gassett did not have the power to keep a study running. Only Braden did.

His mother's involvement in the study might not be enough to sway him. One patient made no difference to a worldwide corporation, and Braden represented that corporation.

Then again, even Braden MacDowell in pursuit of the almighty dollar might not be able to ignore his own mother's needs. Maybe Lana could keep the migraine study going.

I regret to inform you that Plaine Laboratories In-

*ternational has decided to end all trials. Goodbye, Dr.
Donnoli.*

No, that couldn't be the last word between them.

Lana picked up the phone and dialed.

"Excuse me, Mom. I need to take this call."

No matter where he was in the world, Braden's assistant took all his calls, acting as his gatekeeper. She
only picked up on the fifth ring, however, an arrangement that gave Braden the option of answering if he felt
it was necessary. As his phone rang, Braden recognized
the first digits on the caller ID as being from West Central. It could be Jamie calling. Or Quinn. Or...

"MacDowell," he answered on the fourth ring.

"It's Lana. I'd like to set up a meeting. I've got more
information on that migraine trial."

Or it could be his former fiancée, suddenly back in his
life when he'd decided to let the last memory of her go.

"Go ahead," he said, standing up from his mother's
dining-room table and walking into the kitchen.

"I've got availability every day this week. Is there a
particular time that works best for you?"

"I meant, go ahead. I'm listening. Let's hear your
pitch."

"Now?"

He let his silence answer her. Did the woman not
know how business was done? On the spot. At the moment. Around the clock.

"I was calling to set up a future time. We can do this
by phone, if you like, but I wasn't planning on bothering you now, not while you're traveling to Manhattan."

"If I weren't ready to conduct business, I wouldn't
have answered the phone." He didn't say he wasn't on
a plane. He did not tell her he was standing in front of

his mother's kitchen sink, watching through the picture window as twilight settled over the distant barn and the even more distant fence line.

Lana spoke evenly, although he was sure his terse response must have irritated her. "I didn't call to give you a thirty-second canned speech. I am, however, ready to set up a time for the two of us to have an intelligent one-on-one discussion."

Braden heard the steel in her voice. Lana refused to be intimidated by him. She'd never been intimidated by anyone, he recalled.

Good for her. She was going to need that backbone in her new position, but whether or not she had the chops to run West Central's research was not his problem. In fact, West Central was not his problem, not directly. As president, he needed to deal with the big picture, not individual research sites.

"Then when you're ready to present whatever information you feel is necessary," he said, "call Cheryl Gassett. I'm sure her contact info is in Dr. Montgomery's records."

"I realize that the hospital your father founded is no longer worth your time, but I wanted to discuss something that I don't think your regional rep needs to know."

Braden almost smiled. He had to give her points for bringing up his father, a blatant but understandable attempt to stir his emotions. In negotiations, when someone was stonewalling, it was possible to break through that wall by engaging that person's emotions.

Braden had always found it easy to stay detached during business negotiations. Emotions had no place in science. No place in research. Her attempt was useless.

Lana spoke when he did not. "I'm worried about your mother's involvement in this study."

Then again, his mother had no place in research, either. He glanced at her as she entered the kitchen. "My mother is ineligible for the study because she's a relative of a PLI employee. She's not enrolled in any study that I know of."

His mother looked surprised. She pointed to her chest and mouthed the question, *Me?*

Braden raised an eyebrow in question, and she shook her head "no."

"In addition to being a PLI relation, my mother doesn't suffer from migraines, so she wouldn't be enrolled in this study in particular."

"Regardless, she is a patient in the study." Lana's tone was starting to reveal her irritation. Her emotions, at least, were engaged. "She was receiving the active drug, not the placebo. I'm asking you to reconsider. Don't terminate a study that was benefiting your own mother."

"The study is not viable whether my mother is involved in it or not. And she's not."

He looked toward his mother for affirmation, but this time she only used her hand to imitate a phone held to her ear as she mouthed, *Lana?*

Of course, his mother would have keyed in on the name Lana. Braden turned back to the window. He needed to concentrate.

"The address for this Marion MacDowell is your ranch, Braden. She does still live there, doesn't she?"

Braden didn't answer. His mind was racing ahead to the implications of his mother's enrollment in the study.

"If she doesn't suffer from migraines, then why else would she have been given this medicine?"

That was a million-dollar question, indeed. Braden was anxious to get off the phone and find out, but he wasn't going to tell Lana that.

Lana continued probing. "Your parents were friends

with Dr. Montgomery. Would he have been using this study drug to treat your mother for some other reason? What other conditions might it treat?"

Leave it to Lana to figure out the implications so quickly. Braden was burning with curiosity himself. "I'll retrieve the records from your office tomorrow."

"I thought you were in New York."

"My plans changed. I'll be there tomorrow. Eight o'clock."

Braden disconnected the call and turned to his mother. She was quick on the trigger. "Was that Lana Donnoli? Are you two speaking again?"

"First things first, Mom. What kind of pills did Dr. Montgomery give you, and why?"

His mother used her hand to wave his question away, making a shooing motion as if his question were an annoying fly that had gotten in between them when she wanted to talk about something else. "Lana Donnoli, after all these years. I'm happy to hear you two have found each other again."

"Lana and I haven't found anything. We're only speaking out of necessity. I need to know if Dr. Montgomery gave you any pills."

"Out of necessity? What on earth does that mean?"

"It's business," he said firmly. "Let's not get distracted from the subject."

"Lana Donnoli is the subject. Watch your tone, young man."

That did make Braden pause. He was the president of PLI. He set the agendas. If he said the subject was Dr. Montgomery, then that was the subject. One thousand employees of PLI would agree. But his mother?

Braden sighed and let himself lean against the sink. "Dr. Montgomery might have given you a medicine that my company was studying. As my mother, you aren't eligible to be in the study at all. This is serious. Breaches in study protocol can be brought to the FDA's attention."

"By whom? I haven't told a soul."

"There are more people involved. Lana, for one."

"Lana wouldn't tattle on you."

"It's not tattling. This isn't school. This is business. If Lana wanted to use it as a weapon against me—"

"Lana has always been crazy about you. She would do no such thing."

Braden's phone was on the third ring. He answered it. "MacDowell."

"Yes, I know. You hung up on me, Braden."

Lana sounded angry. Her emotions were engaged, so Braden should have the upper hand. There was, however, nothing to negotiate, certainly nothing that needed to be discussed while his mother glared at him.

"I didn't hang up on you. We'd concluded our business and we'll meet tomorrow." He emphasized the word *business* for his mother's benefit. Dang, but she could still give him a look that made him want to squirm. He had an angry woman standing in front of him and an angry woman speaking in his ear. The president of PLI was not quite in control of the situation, and he knew it.

"Braden, I cannot turn any records over to you at eight in the morning."

"They aren't your records. They belong to PLI."

"I'm well aware that your company owns the data."

"Then you'll return it upon demand. That's part of every contract."

"You can demand all you like, but that won't make my office door magically unlock at eight o'clock. My assistant won't be in yet, and she's the only one who knows where everything is, including the door's key. I've only been in town for a day."

That was an easy problem to solve. He couldn't believe Lana needed instructions. "Tell her to come in early."

He hung up, then rubbed his forehead, mostly to break eye contact with his mother.

"That was Lana again?" she asked. "Be nice. I told you that girl was crazy about you."

"That girl is not crazy about me. That girl is only speaking to me because she is the head of research at West Central."

"Since when?"

"Since this morning, apparently. I pulled a million dollars of funding from her today. A million dollars can make people desperate, Mom, and if she wanted to create problems for me with the FDA, she could."

"She won't."

"I'm glad you have such confidence in my ex-fiancée."

His mother narrowed her eyes.

He hoped he looked innocent. *No, Ma, I wasn't being a smart aleck. Honest.*

Braden tried again. "Even if Lana keeps your involvement a secret to the grave, I still need to know why you were being given a migraine medicine."

"I don't get migraines."

"Exactly. The salient question is, what *do* you get that Dr. Montgomery was trying to treat?"

"I know you are a doctor, but I'll tell you what I've told your brothers. You are not *my* doctor."

Despite the topic, his mother was smiling—or rather, trying not to smile. The corners of her mouth were twitching.

Braden's bafflement warred with impatience. "What is amusing you? This is serious."

"If you say so, son. Lana Donnoli is back in town, and you want to bring a guest out here for Valentine's weekend."

"Not Lana." Good God, not Lana. Not that heartbreak. His mother had it all wrong.

"Grab a dish towel." She started scrubbing the pan she'd used to make his chicken-fried steak. "Better yet, go on back to town and see your Lana."

"It's business. She can wait until morning."

She only smiled. "No son of mine would ever be so rude to a lady over the phone."

"I wasn't rude. I was businesslike."

"I'm sorry to spoil your surprise, but I can put two and two together. Lana calls, and you leave the room. When I follow, you pretend to be angry with her and hang up. Tonight, you can't stay at the ranch, because you are sleeping at the Four Seasons. Here, give me that dish towel and go on to your hotel."

"No, that isn't—"

The mother who was supposedly so frail put her hand on his shoulder and gave him a shove toward the door. "I'm delighted that you and Lana are back together. Valentine's will be wonderful. You don't have to tell her I figured it out. I'll act surprised."

"You'll be surprised because Lana Donnoli is not the woman I'm planning on marrying."

She escorted him all the way to the front door, forcing him out of his own childhood home in the gentlest way possible. "Marriage? You're going to announce a marriage? Sweetheart, that is so romantic. Now go. Lana's waiting, and I can't stand to listen to another of these fake fights on your phone."

Braden realized his phone was ringing. He checked the screen. It was indeed Lana. He let it ring. She could chat with his assistant this time.

"Mom, don't get your hopes up like this. You'll be disappointed."

"Right. Mum's the word. I'll be surprised, I promise. Good night, sweetheart."

Braden had barely gotten his rental car started when his phone vibrated again. It was laughable that his mother thought he might need to fake a phone fight with Lana. They'd had plenty of real ones, burning up the line from Boston to Austin, back in the day. He waited for the fifth ring that would cue his assistant to answer, then enjoyed the silence while he began the long drive down the ranch road.

The phone rang again within seconds.

For the love of—

His emotions were engaged now. This negotiation was breaking down. Phone calls with Lana always had been disastrous.

He answered without taking his eyes off the long ranch road. "Give it a rest, Lana. I'm not going to argue with you all night. Those days are long over."

There was a moment of silence, which Braden imagined meant Lana was suitably subdued by his show of temper.

A woman's voice finally spoke. "Lana? Who is Lana?"

Braden let his eyes flick to the screen, although it was unnecessary. Of course, the name and thumbnail photo of Claudia St. James were displayed in full color.

"I'm sorry, Claudia. It was nothing. A business call."

"It didn't sound like a business call. Who is Lana?"

Braden sighed in defeat. The drive into Austin was going to be a long one.

Chapter Six

The patients enrolled in PLI's migraine study might not suffer from high blood pressure, but Lana was pretty sure hers was going through the roof.

She glared at her phone's screen. Braden wasn't going to return her last call, obviously. His executive assistant had sounded excruciatingly cool and competent, so Lana knew her message hadn't been lost. Braden's workday was apparently over, although his assistant's obviously was not. Poor woman.

Well, Lana was no slave driver. She wasn't going to call her own assistant this late at night and demand that Myrna rearrange her schedule to be here at eight in the morning, no matter what Braden demanded. Her blood pressure hiked up another millimeter just thinking about it.

She ought to lock the office door and go home. Braden could show up tomorrow at the time of his choosing, but she wouldn't be here. He could stew in the hallway, calling her number in vain. Since not-for-profit hospitals didn't provide their department chairs with twenty-four-hour assistants like Braden had, he'd be stuck listening to her voice mail. Even better.

The whole scenario sounded wonderfully vengeful—but Lana knew it was a fantasy. She wouldn't do it. This wasn't about her personal irritation; this was about patients who were suffering.

She had some sleuthing to do, stat. It was nearing midnight, and she needed to find a link between Marion MacDowell and the other enrollees. All patients had listed their other medical conditions upon entering the study. Lana had sorted those lists every which way, but nothing striking had appeared, no similarities in secondary diseases beyond the migraines.

Her stomach growled. She'd intended to battle her exhaustion only long enough to call Braden, set up a future appointment and then go home. Her new apartment was full of cardboard boxes. The headboard and rails of her bed were propped against the wall, unassembled, so her mattress was flat on the floor. Her great ambition for the evening had been to locate the box containing her microwave oven, heat up an organic frozen dinner and then flop onto that mattress for the night.

Instead, Braden had insisted that West Central return its data to PLI. She would have to wait one more day before giving in to her exhaustion. Patients were counting on her.

The rush of adrenaline was welcome. Knowing she'd be seeing Braden again in a matter of hours made her feel energized. Not because she was looking forward to seeing him, but because she was in competition with him.

She had to beat Braden at his own game. The challenge was better than coffee.

"All right, Dr. Montgomery," she murmured into the silence of her office. "Why did you put Marion Mac-Dowell on this drug?"

She tapped her pencil at the corner of her mouth. Perhaps she needed to look at Marion MacDowell's involvement from a fresh angle. The medicine may have been designed to treat migraines, but an unusual side effect might have been reported. Sometimes, a prospective medicine had a side effect that turned out to be more beneficial than the original effect. A prospective asthma medicine, for example, might unexpectedly cause low blood sugar and become a diabetes medication. It was a rare occurrence, but it happened.

Perhaps Dr. Montgomery had noticed that PLI's migraine drug was causing an unusual but beneficial side effect, one that could benefit Marion MacDowell in some way.

It was a long shot.

It was also nearly midnight.

Lana started looking for frequently reported side effects of the study. At least one hundred patients had been enrolled during the six months before Dr. Montgomery had given the last slot to his friend. Lana began sorting her list again, this time by date of enrollment, then copying the side-effect data for only the first six months' worth of patients, then...

An hour later, she glared at her still-dark phone screen. So far, she'd found nothing. At this rate, it was quite possible she'd still be here at eight in the morning, still wearing the same dress from today's meeting. Braden would know she'd pulled an all-nighter.

She doubted he'd be shocked. They'd pulled more all-nighters together than she could count during residency. Having Braden by her side had made those years an adventure. They'd met every challenge together. Lana and Braden versus the evil attending physicians. Lana and Braden conquering forty-eight-hour workdays. Lana and Braden slipping into the storage room.

She closed her eyes for a moment and let her head rest on the tall back of Dr. Montgomery's oversized leather desk chair. When she opened her eyes again, Braden was there, standing on the other side of the glass door, framed by pink paper hearts.

She was dreaming.

Braden opened the door without knocking.

She was not dreaming.

"What are you doing here?" he demanded.

Lana stood immediately. Her pumps had been kicked off long ago, so jumping to her feet didn't do much for her, size-wise. Braden walked past Myrna's desk to stand before hers, hands on his hips, glaring down at her as if she were a disobedient child.

She was no child. "This is my office. I'm the one who gets to ask what you're doing here."

"I was just walking past the door," he said, frowning at her. "Your lights were on."

"At midnight, you just happened to be walking down this hallway of West Central?"

"Yes. My brother had a late dinner break, so I came by to see him." He crossed his arms over his chest. He'd changed into a soft knit shirt and jeans, she noticed, the same clothes he'd always preferred, even when she and all the other residents were living in scrubs.

Jeans or not, he hadn't come to pull an all-nighter by her side. He was having dinner with his brother. It wasn't his job to find a reason to keep pentagab viable.

He got to sit back, relax and wait for someone else to make the case for him.

Must be nice.

"While you were having dinner, I was working on pentagab."

He only raised one eyebrow at her. "That's not a particularly wise way to spend your time. The drug is dead."

The man was a broken record on the subject. She threw her hands up. "Aren't you the least bit curious about why your mother was taking it?"

"You're investigating my mother right now?"

"I only have until eight in the morning, since you refused to change your schedule." She pinned him with a look, and for once, he looked away first. "I haven't figured out why Montgomery gave it to your mother yet, but I've eliminated a few possibilities. It's nothing cardiovascular, for example."

"Let me see what you've got." Braden stepped around her desk, crowding her personal space, leaning in to see her computer screen, practically forcing her out from behind her own desk.

They brushed arms. His forearms were bare. His skin was warm, the muscles underneath firm. His whole body was intimidating, too large and vivid after being only a memory, only a broken dream for so long. Lana felt... well, she felt...

She felt indignant, that was what she felt. How dare this man walk into her office and take over?

She pushed her shoulder in between him and her desk, reaching for her monitor and shutting it off with a press of a button. She faced him squarely. He didn't step back.

"Eight in the morning, Braden. We have a meeting at eight, and until then, I'm not ready to present anything to you. In the meantime, your manners are appalling."

"My *what*?"

"Do you always barge into other people's offices and help yourself to their desks?"

Lana could have stood there forever, watching him splutter, enjoying his speechless moment. The man had apparently been treated with too much deference for too long. It was gratifying to the extreme to be the one to remind Mr. Millionaire Mogul that manners still mattered.

He gestured around her, toward her monitor. "That's my data, and if I want to—"

She cut him off, literally going toe-to-toe with him, heedless that her toes were bare. "It is West Central's data, and until I present it to PLI, I can study it any way I want to, for as long as I want to, for any reason I want to."

She was so close, she could see the way his pupils widened briefly. He loomed over her. "And that's what you want?"

The backs of her legs were against her desk. To put any distance between them, she'd have to lean backward, practically lie on her own desk. Their position suddenly seemed sexual, the air charged with possibilities that should never, ever feel so tempting. She spoke through clenched teeth. "It's what I want. So back off."

Or else kiss me.

The words popped into her head, crystal clear. Alarming.

Abruptly, Braden turned away from her. He stood with his back to her, hands on his hips again. Although she could not detect the slightest tremor in him, although nothing about his posture appeared anything less than commanding, she had the intuition that Braden felt unsteady.

So did she.

He spoke quietly. "You're looking into my mother's health. It's not cardiovascular, you said."

"N-no. It doesn't appear to be so." Lana felt like a fool. Of course, the man was worried about his only remaining parent. That was why Braden was so intense tonight. She'd leapt to the conclusion that his emotions were for her. Worse, she'd assumed it was sexual attraction, that the man still could find her irresistible after all these years, when he was actually worried for his mother.

Humbled, she turned the monitor back on. "Do you know why Montgomery wanted her to have this drug?"

He turned around to face her. "She won't tell me."

Lana sighed. "That's a shame. It would save me a lot of time if she would. I'm looking for a needle in a haystack."

Braden walked around to the opposite side of the desk, where any other visitor to her office would have stood. "Were you planning on staying here all night until you found it?"

"It was one way to be sure the door was unlocked at eight, at least."

Braden looked at her in surprise for a moment. She knew the moment he realized she was needling him, because one corner of his mouth turned up in the beginnings of a grin. "We could work together. An all-nighter, like old times."

He remembered. She felt a pang in her heart, a bittersweet beat.

The ghost of a grin disappeared from Braden's lips. "You've already pulled a few all-nighters this week, haven't you? You look like you're about to drop. When's the last time you ate?"

She couldn't remember when she'd eaten last. There'd been some dry cereal when she'd gotten dressed in the morning, because she hadn't remembered to buy milk yet. Myrna had offered her a Danish at some point today.

Braden strode to her office door with a soft curse under his breath and yanked it open. "You always took your 'patients first' mantra too far. Go home, Lana. Eat. Get some sleep."

She only stood there, memories rushing through her. Braden had always been the one to make sure she didn't overdo it. She'd always been the one willing to run on adrenaline alone, willing to sacrifice everything. Everything.

Braden kept holding the door open, but he looked as if he was ready to bodily force her through it. "Haven't you learned anything in six years? You're human like the rest of us. You can't run forever without food and sleep. Go home."

Oh, but she had learned something. She'd learned more about herself than she'd wanted to. Her *patients first* mantra had been a facade back then, something she'd spouted to justify the hours she put in. The real reason she had worked longer and harder than anyone else in their residency program wasn't to take care of patients. It was to prove she was the best.

Patients first had meant *I'm the most dedicated resident in this program.* Lana knew that now, but back then, she'd kept pushing herself, believing it was the only way to be a great physician, until she'd met Braden MacDowell. His father had founded this very hospital, but Braden said he'd also taught him how to ride a horse and build a campfire. Lana had started to let herself believe she could be a great doctor and still have fun, with Braden by her side.

Then Braden had gone away.

Without Braden to keep her in check, her drive to be

the best had cost her everything. She'd worked herself to exhaustion, she'd miscarried their accidental pregnancy, and her life had never been the same.

Patients first meant something different now. Lana wasn't pulling an all-nighter because she thought she was better than the other residents, or even because her department couldn't afford to lose a million dollars. She genuinely wanted those children in D.C. to keep getting pentagab, and there was no one except her to make that happen.

If she let Braden boss her into leaving, if she left to eat and sleep and focus on her own needs, then hundreds of children in D.C. would lose their study medicine.

Lana stood her ground while Braden held the door. "If I leave now, will you keep the study going until I have a chance to finish this analysis? Your mother and everyone else will keep their medicine?"

"The study was canceled today. You can leave because you won't find anything that makes pentagab suddenly start working for migraines."

"Not for adults, I agree. But for the pediatric study, will you keep that one going while I try to find out what is happening with your mother?"

"Possibly. We'll talk tomorrow."

"But—"

"Tomorrow. Not at eight o'clock. Sleep in. I can't negotiate with someone who's half-dead."

Lana turned her monitor off once more. The pediatric study might live another day. The possibility of victory made her drop her guard. As she passed Braden on her way out, she said, "You can't be half-dead. Either you're dead or you're not. You can't have it both ways."

He was silent for a moment, for a fraction of a second, but it was long enough for Lana to want to kick herself for falling into their old game of pointing out oxymorons to one another.

"It would take a minor miracle," Braden murmured. Then he turned and walked away, leaving her alone as she locked the door from the inside, stepped into the hall and pulled it shut behind her.

She was nearly to her car before his oxymoron hit her: a minor miracle. A miracle couldn't be minor; it could only be, well, miraculous.

The pang in her heart didn't catch her by surprise this time. Braden had remembered their old game, but that didn't mean her old fiancé was her new friend. He'd given pentagab and her pediatric patients only a single day's reprieve. The ruthless businessman couldn't turn back into the caring physician she'd once loved.

It would take a minor miracle.

The heavily used trail around Lady Bird Lake was dotted with humans of all shapes and sizes. College students who ran with effortless youth. Hipsters who sat on rock walls and shared earbuds. Children who were too slow, middle-aged couples who drifted from one side of the path to the other as they conducted business on their phones and elderly people on a mission to stay fit. Braden passed them all as he ran, dodging each human obstacle as he pounded through Zilker Park in the afternoon sun.

The temperate Austin winter hadn't kept anyone away. Braden veered right to pass a cluster of seniors, then straight ahead to thread the space between two young men who ran fast, but not faster than Braden. He was driven by the need to leave them all behind, as if by clearing all these obstacles on the reddish-brown, packed-earth path, he'd clear all the obstacles that had suddenly appeared in his life.

"Are we in a race I don't know about?"

Quinn sounded angry. Braden slowed down. He shouldn't leave his brother behind, not after he'd asked Quinn to meet him for a workout. A lap around the park with his brother had seemed necessary for his sanity.

The morning had started with a bang. An Austin city official had leaked word of the PLI research facilities. Braden had demanded explanations from the key players, and then he'd debriefed the rest of PLI's research division over secured cyber connections. Afterward, he'd had to countermand his own order to cancel the pentagab study, thanks to his mother's involvement and Lana's interference. Determined to stay on his schedule, he'd visited the specific jeweler in Austin he'd had in mind, but none of the engagement rings seemed right for Claudia, an illogical and absurd problem that had dogged him in New York, as well.

To top it off, Claudia herself was calling him with an almost creepy frequency, demanding to know exactly why he hadn't returned to New York when he'd planned to. Braden wanted to marry Claudia because she was independent and stable, yet last night's one lousy phone call, his one mention of the name Lana, had caused Claudia to morph into a neurotic, suspicious person.

"What the hell?" Quinn yelled from behind him.

Braden slowed down just enough for Quinn to come alongside him again. "Bad day," he said, hoping that sufficed as an apology.

Quinn grunted, as if that explanation made perfect sense.

They ran in sync and in silence for several strides. They were nearly back to the parking lot where they'd left Quinn's motorcycle and Braden's rented sports car, and hard breathing kept the conversation short and to the point.

"Personal bad day," Quinn asked between strides, "or professional?"

"Both."

"Need help?"

"I wish."

It wasn't Quinn's problem that when the jeweler had asked Braden which ring reflected his bride's personality, Claudia's image hadn't come to mind. Braden had pictured Lana, damn it, Lana in a shop on their lunch break, wearing scrubs and modeling white veils for him. Every time he'd said he liked one, she'd plucked it off and laughed, assuring him it was not the one she'd already bought and hidden from him, so they wouldn't face bad luck if he saw her in it before their wedding day.

He wondered what her veil would have looked like. He'd never seen it. Had she returned it to the shop after she'd dropped the ring in the mail?

What the hell did it matter?

Braden sprinted, full out, the rest of the way to the finish.

He was still bent over, hands on his knees and gulping air, when Quinn jogged past him to flop on the bench of a picnic table. He stretched his arms across the battered green boards of the table. "Well, that was fun."

Braden stood up tall, walked a few steps away and kicked at the base of an oak tree. "Why did you hire Lana?"

Quinn gave him the Dad look, the lift of one eyebrow. "It was Montgomery's idea."

"It was a bad one."

"Not for West Central. Lana was a hell of a bargain. She's going to help our bottom line more than Montgomery did or ever would. Speaking of bottom lines, I realize that West Central is probably an insignificant slice of your portfolio, but did you read the annual report?"

There it was again, that subtle implication that Braden no longer cared about things the rest of the MacDowells cared about. "It was Dad's hospital. Of course I read the report."

"And?"

The fact that Quinn would ask sent a red flag up in Braden's mind. "It looked fine. Fairly robust for the current state of hospitals. You didn't think so?"

"I wanted the board to call the CEO in for more details. He needs to account for some of those numbers."

"What did the rest of the board say?"

"They have happy ears. They heard the CEO say what they wanted to hear." With an angry push on the planks of the picnic table, Quinn got to his feet. "Montgomery's a sloppy bookkeeper at best, so when he recommended Lana, I didn't think twice. I know she's meticulous. Ethical. It was easy for me to endorse her to the rest of the board. I'm sorry if it's caused a problem for you, though."

Braden shook off his concern, but he had nothing to say. He didn't know what the problem was himself.

"You two have a fight?" Quinn asked.

"Nope." Braden squinted up at the remains of a kite, still stuck in the leafless branches of a tree long after the annual kite festival had passed. "I'm buying Claudia a ring."

"The woman I met in New York?" Quinn half sat on the edge of the table and crossed his arms over his chest, showing all the signs of settling in for a longer discussion.

It was undeniably gratifying. Braden hadn't been

home for more than a few days every year, but his brother was still his brother. "She's the one. Thought I'd do it at the ranch, over Valentine's weekend. I want to ask her in front of the family. Last time, with Lana, it was all private. We kept it a secret for a few months, you know, before we let the rest of the world in on it."

"No, I didn't know that."

"I don't want to make the same mistakes twice. I don't want this ring returned."

"What exactly was that mistake?" Acting as if it were an everyday question, Quinn started untying his shoe, because he'd threaded his motorcycle's key through the laces.

In the business world, in Braden's world, when mistakes occurred, they were analyzed. There were after action reports, recommendations to modify business practices, steps taken to ensure that the same mistake was never repeated. But with his first engagement, Braden had gotten none of that. Lana had simply decided she didn't want him for a husband after all, and he had no idea why.

That had to explain why he was so crippled when it came to picking out an engagement ring for Claudia. She seemed perfect for him, but Lana had seemed perfect for him also, once upon a time. He'd given Lana his heart and soul. He couldn't pour those resources into another losing proposition.

He was a businessman who never made the same mistake twice, and until he learned exactly what had gone wrong the first time, he didn't risk a second commitment.

"I'm asking because I really don't remember why you two broke up," Quinn said. "Where did you and Lana go wrong?"

Braden clapped his brother on the shoulder. "That is

an excellent question. I'm spending one more night in town. Lana has owed me an answer for six years, and tonight, I'm going to get it."

Chapter Seven

It's a business meeting, not a date.

Still, Lana opened every cardboard wardrobe box in her newly rented apartment, looking for the perfect outfit to wear for dinner with Braden. Dinner together as professionals, not as old lovers who hadn't seen one another in years. Not as that, no matter what Myrna believed.

Her assistant had delivered the short message from Braden: *Viejo Mundo, eight o'clock.* Then Myrna had given Lana a rave review of the latest restaurant to enter Austin's already-impressive restaurant scene.

"A date at Viejo Mundo is something special, Dr. Donnoli."

"It's not a date, but it better be something special. Our department is going to be hurting unless I hit a home run tonight."

"A home run?" Myrna, gray-haired and grandmotherly, had giggled. "When I was your age, nice girls didn't go past first base on a first date—but it's not your first date with Dr. MacDowell, is it?"

"He prefers Mr. MacDowell, and this is strictly business."

The problem was, none of Lana's business attire seemed suitable. She opened her last cardboard box and pulled out a high-collared dress. Too stuffy. He might think she'd become a dried-up old prune since she'd left him.

Maybe true, but he doesn't need to know.

She let a camisole slip dress slide to the floor. Too sexy. He might assume she was trying to find a bed partner for the night.

Not true, but he pretty much ruined me for any other man. He definitely didn't need to know that.

In the end, she settled on that time-honored standby, the little black dress, worn with her hair down, her makeup carefully natural and her jewelry subtle. Professional. Her shoes were low-heeled pumps, practical in case she got called in to cover for a physician at the hospital.

Her portfolio was filled with two copies of all the research assets she'd compiled. Her mission tonight was twofold. Not only did she need to keep pentagab alive, but she needed to nail down another study—or two, or three—with PLI this year. Business news channels had been buzzing today with rumors that PLI would build their own research facilities right here in Austin. Her department needed to get all the contracts and all the funding they could before that happened.

As she dressed for dinner, she felt alive in a way she hadn't felt in ages, which she took as a positive sign that she'd made the right choice to change jobs. The prospect of negotiating with the president of PLI tonight was exciting in a way her career in D.C. had never been. The fact that the president in question was Braden MacDowell was unfortunate, but so far, they'd managed to interact in a professional manner. Mostly.

Lana had to drive herself to the restaurant, further proof that this was not a date. But when she arrived, the hostess started leading her past clusters of tables, all candlelit like a mysterious Mayan fantasy, until it became obvious that Lana was being led to a table for two, tucked into an alcove. It was semiprivate, just the table, two chairs and a window with the dark night beyond.

Braden had already arrived, looking terribly handsome in the dim lighting that would make reading her spreadsheets difficult. He was wearing a business suit again—or had been. His jacket was discarded over the back of his chair. His tie was missing. His sleeves had been turned up a few times, exposing wrists and forearms. When he stood to pull out her chair, the polished cotton of his shirt slid over the muscles of his shoulders.

She knew just how he would look, shrugging out of that shirt and tossing it onto their bed.

The hostess reached behind Lana to put the menus on the table, forcing her to inch closer to Braden. It was intimate, this closeness, bringing instant awareness of how athletic he was. How physical he'd always been, raised on a ranch, a lover of sports. A lover of her.

This setting was much too much like an intimate date. That, she couldn't allow. Her heart needed shielding from Braden, and tonight, her career was going to provide it.

"Hello, Braden." Staying on her feet, Lana offered him her hand for a polite handshake, pasting her best let's-get-down-to-business smile on her face.

Braden shook her hand, of course, since she'd stuck it out in front of him, but he didn't let go of it. She could feel his gaze on the skin her dress left bare. Her arms, her legs, her modest décolletage. The collar of his shirt was unbuttoned, exposing a tanned throat. She'd snuggled the side of her face into him there a hundred times.

She'd known him for years. She'd worn his ring. And for six weeks, she'd been accidentally pregnant with his child.

Business. That was why she was here. Not to stir up old memories and old hurts. She seated herself, dismissed the hostess with a polite smile and prepared to steer the conversation.

"Thank you for meeting with me. I'm glad we were able to set this up before you returned to New York. I needed this day to get a handle on my department's—"

"I won't be living in New York full-time. I'll be commuting from here."

"So the rumors today were accurate? PLI will be building a research center here in Austin?"

He gave her an impersonal, professional smile. "I can neither confirm nor deny those rumors at this time. Wall Street will just have to keep guessing."

It was surreal, to know that her ex had the power to influence a company's value on the stock market. "If the rumors turn out to be true, congratulations. It will be wonderful news for the city of Austin. Your company has a reputation for excellence."

She let the professional platitudes roll off her tongue, but failed to stop when a personal thought entered her stream of consciousness. "I'm sure your mother will be pleased that you'll be home more often."

And how awful for Lana, to wonder if she'd run into him every time she left the apartment. She'd taken the position at West Central knowing that Braden MacDowell was headquartered in Manhattan. It was too late to reconsider. Her pulse picked up speed at the thought of seeing Braden again and again after tonight, around town, around the hospital.

He watched her intently. "Did you learn anything new about my mother's involvement in the pentagab study?"

And by that, she knew he meant *is my mother seriously ill?*

"No, I'm sorry. Not yet."

"Don't drag your feet on it."

Her moment of sympathy ended in a flash. "I find it offensive that you'd even suggest such a thing. Patients are depending on me. They need this drug—" She cut herself short, caught in the middle of her old *patients first* mantra.

"Patients like my mother, for one."

"You can't think I would drag my feet because your mother is involved?"

His silence was telling.

It hurt her terribly. No wonder he'd let their engagement end without a fight. He assumed she was the lowest kind of person. Maybe last night she'd entertained a little thought of petty revenge—*let him stand in the hallway in front of a locked door*—but that hardly meant she'd let a woman's health decline just because that woman was related to her ex.

Wounded, Lana explained herself as forcefully as she could without raising her voice in the quiet restaurant. "It's because Marion is involved that I found the time today to rule out another class of side effects—pentagab has practically no dermatologic effects, you should be happy to know—and I find it extremely offensive that you think I would ever let Marion suffer from a mystery illness if I could help it. I wouldn't let anyone suffer, let alone—"

At the start of her defense, Braden had almost instantly held up a palm, and he was still making a slow-down motion.

Lana rushed on. "—let alone someone I care about personally. The fact that the patient in question is your mother is more likely to motivate me than deter me. Marion was always—she was always—"

Lana paused to struggle for the words to describe a woman who'd treated her like the daughter she had not become. Marion was the perfect mother in Lana's eyes, the kind of mother she could never be: self-sacrificing, devoted to her family to the exclusion of all else. A good mother. An ideal mother.

"Marion was always *lovely* to me. I would never use her to get to you. I wouldn't use any patient's suffering for—"

"I get it. Patients come first for Lana Donnoli, even when they are related to me."

Especially when they are related to you.

She'd known it today, as the columns of numbers and letters had danced on the page before her eyes, that she was trying to help Braden. She never wanted to make his life harder, only easier. Still. Their engagement had left that indelible mark in her heart.

Braden touched her portfolio with one dismissive tap of his finger. "You realize that when you're done with that analysis, I'll kill the study. Even the pediatric one."

She lifted her chin. "We'll see."

"There's nothing to see. That drug does not work in adult migraines. There's no saving something ineffective. Unless..." He began slowly shaking his head at her. "Unless the brilliant Lana Donnoli, smartest kid in the class, finds something no one else has. My God, Lana, are you still trying to be Superwoman? You've taken it on your shoulders to single-handedly save a drug, haven't you? You don't even work for the company that makes it."

"I don't see why you are getting angry about this."

"Waste makes me angry. You are wasting your effort to prove that pentagab works for something, anything, in the adult population so that it will be available for that tiny amount of pediatric migraine sufferers. You are that stubborn."

"Since you are so concerned about dollars and cents, I would think you'd be delighted that you've got me working for free on the PLI payroll."

"I know you, Lana. You'll sacrifice sleep and food and everything else, trying to make it happen."

"So what? That won't hurt you this time."

This time.

Lana abruptly fell silent, horrified that those words had slipped out. This time, there would be no consequences if she overdid it. But once, it had cost Braden a chance at fatherhood. She knew it, even if he did not.

This time, and every time for the rest of her life, she could work as long and as hard as she liked, and miss as many meals as she could stand, and there would be nothing for Braden to lose. If the work in question benefited PLI, then he could only profit.

"Did you review the derm effects before or after you got some sleep? Did you sleep at all?"

"Yes, I did, but it's irrelevant."

"Good. It was always murder to get you to stop long enough to take a nap."

Oh, but he had stopped her. He'd been very effective about getting her into bed. They'd make love, an afternoon interlude, a savoring of bare skin sliding on bare skin, and then she'd sleep like a baby.

Her gaze dropped to his throat again, to the skin revealed where the tie was missing. The man looked good in candlelight.

This was all wrong. She'd prepared for a business meeting, but here they were in a restaurant, sparring about her work habits, almost as if they were a couple. One had to love someone to argue with them about the hours they put into their job. Braden had once loved her, but that had died a long time ago. When he'd accepted the return of her ring, he'd lost the right to berate her work habits.

"I appreciate your concern, Braden. West Central will return accurate data on pentagab within the week, and I assure you the statistical analysis won't suffer because one person in the research department failed to get adequate rest. Let's move on. When Myrna delivered your message today, I took the opportunity to prepare a list of West Central's assets."

"In one day."

"Yes. Like I said in the conference room yesterday, I'd like to give PLI the right of first refusal. We've got a lot to offer."

"You can speak to Cheryl Gassett about that."

"But this is why we're here."

The waitress chose that moment to introduce herself. Lana pasted a polite look on her face as she churned inside.

"We're not ready to order," Braden said to the smiling young woman.

Lana didn't bother opening her menu as the waitress left. "Why would I deal with Cheryl when you're right here, right now?"

"I'm one of the presidents of PLI, Lana. West Central is too small for me to personally work with."

"Yesterday, it wasn't too small. You took the meeting, not this Cheryl Gassett."

"I wanted to see West Central again. I used the migraine study as my excuse. I needed to go back there one more time."

Lana refused to ask why. The reason was going to be something personal, something to do with her. She wasn't ready for this. Any one of a dozen Pandora's boxes could open. She'd only come tonight for work.

"Fine," she said briskly. "I'll contact her. While PLI is in the process of building, I assume Cheryl will still consider West Central until the new facilities are viable?" If she'd learned nothing else in the past forty-eight hours, she'd learned that Braden wanted things to be viable.

"We have more important ground to cover."

She opened her portfolio and called upon her training as a physician to operate dispassionately. Her voice was emotionless when she spoke. "Braden, I came here prepared to work with you. Nothing more."

"I need more. I want to know where things went wrong, six years ago."

She sat back, stunned.

Braden was direct. "The last time I spoke to you was over the phone. We were seventeen hundred miles apart, and you were sobbing—"

"No." She refused to have this discussion. She was wild to avoid it. "The last time we spoke was in my office, around midnight. You canceled our eight o'clock meeting, then you scheduled this dinner through my assistant. Here we are." She slid one set of papers toward Braden. "I'm sure it will be at least a year before PLI can complete the building, and in the meanwhile, West Central can offer—"

"You were sobbing, damn it, and you wouldn't let me say anything then, either."

"This isn't the time or place."

"It's now or never, for me. There are things I need to know. That last phone call from you was too short, and too confusing, and too important."

Alarm made her turn in her seat, angling toward the door.

"And so help me, Lana, if you leave this restaurant, I'll follow you. And then we'll have this conversation in the parking lot. Your choice."

"You lured me here," she accused, feeling trapped. "You had no intention of doing business with West Central at all."

"As you so astutely began to point out to me, PLI will need to use existing facilities while our own are being built. Don't worry, Dr. Donnoli. Your precious research department will be duly analyzed as a possibility for all appropriately targeted studies."

He had the absolute gall to slap the papers back onto her portfolio, close the folder and set it on the window ledge next to their table. "Now, I'd like to speak to Lana, the woman I once planned to marry."

"She's not available."

He leaned the smallest bit over the table, and she gave herself away by inching back.

"You owe me this," he said.

"I owe you?" Like a dam breaking after days of strain, the words rushed out of her. "You are the one who left me. You left Texas, and you left your training as a physician, and you left me. All at once."

He sat back at her words, doing a fine imitation of a man who was amazed. Words seemed to escape him for a moment as he shook his head in disbelief. "Is that how you've twisted it for yourself? All this time, you've been painting yourself as the injured party?"

"I am the—I *was* the injured party."

"I never left you. I never gave up on us. That was all you, Lana."

Their table was in an alcove, but it wasn't completely private. The diners at the nearest table turned their heads at their emphatic statements.

Lana lowered her voice. "You moved to Boston instead of starting our life together in Texas."

"I moved to Boston temporarily, to get my MBA from one of the best schools in the world."

"Two years, you would've been gone."

"Two years, while you were working hundred-hour weeks as chief resident. We wouldn't have seen each other, anyway."

"We would have if you'd been working at the hospital, too, like we'd planned."

"I didn't want to be a doctor, Lana." He practically ground his words out through clenched teeth. "How many times can I tell you? I knew in our second year of residency that I wouldn't be happy as a physician, but by then I'd put so much effort into it, I was wise enough to finish the program."

"I never heard any of those doubts during that second year. Not until we were well into our third year, and already engaged."

He looked away from her at that, silent for a moment as he rubbed his jaw. Lana felt a little satisfaction that she'd gotten him to look away first.

"I didn't complain during the second year, because that's when I fell in love with you," he said, gazing out the dark window. And then, even more quietly, "Wild horses wouldn't have driven me away."

Her heart hurt all over again at the reminder of what it had been like to be loved by this man. To be a priority in his life.

He turned to her again. "But by the third year, I knew that I couldn't live an entire lifetime in the wrong career, even with you by my side."

"But you finished your residency, anyway, and then you wasted it. You would have been a great doctor, and you wasted it."

"No—you would have been a great doctor. I'm sure you *are* a great doctor. You love everything about it. You have a calling for it. I didn't."

"We both graduated in the top ten percent of our class."

He made a dismissive gesture. "Because I'm smart, Lana. Just like you. I didn't say I couldn't have been a doctor academically or technically. But being smart would not have made me a great doctor where it counts— in the treatment room, one-on-one with the patient."

Lana sat back in her chair. "So instead of working with me, the fiancée you'd promised to spend the rest of your life with, you left."

"I went to get an education in the area where I wanted to apply my talents. Med school had always been my parents' idea, not mine. They had this picture in their heads of all three of their sons becoming doctors, just like Dad. They groomed us for it for as long as I can remember. They got their way—they could tell their friends I'm a doctor, because technically I am, but I'm leaving the actual doctoring up to Quinn and Jamie."

Another little arrow lodged in her heart at the names of his two brothers. When she'd lost Braden, she'd lost his family, too, including the two men who had already accepted her as their sister. Braden had changed his mind about their future, and that had changed everything. Everything.

"You knew I wanted us to start a practice together," she said, resentment fresh inside her. "We'd talked about buying Dr. Forrest's practice from him when he retired."

"You knew I was applying to MBA programs throughout that final year of residency. I was wise enough by then to know that we'd be happier in the long run if we were each satisfied with our careers."

It had dimmed her happiness, though. The future they'd planned together was no longer adequate. Resentment had made its ugly entry into their relationship, and she hadn't known how to prevent it, not when being a physician was still considered good enough for her, but no longer good enough for Braden Mac-Dowell.

And then I got pregnant; that didn't fit into anyone's plan.

She'd loved him madly. Deeply. Yet he'd become no more than a voice on a phone line while she held a positive pregnancy test in her hand.

She couldn't say such a thing out loud, not after years of silence, so Braden continued speaking.

"I thought a two-year sacrifice would pay off in decades of happiness with you. A long-distance relationship was going to be hard, but I knew what I felt for you wasn't going to change in two years."

"Well, it's been six years now, not two. Feelings did change, didn't they?"

She said it as more of a statement than a question, but she was suddenly aware that the answer wasn't necessarily clear. There was something in the way he was looking at her in the flickering candlelight. Something in his voice, as if the hurt and the emotion were still raw for him.

"Didn't they?" she repeated and held her breath.

"Lana, I…" Again, he looked away from her, out the window, into the night. "Lana, there's another woman. It's been six years. Six years. I went to the jeweler to buy her a ring. I thought it was the right thing to do."

To get down on one knee again? To open a little velvet box and make a woman's heart stop with your declaration of undying love?

He'd already done that once, in a hospital's chapel. For her. And she'd believed every word. Somewhere in her heart, a little piece of her still believed he'd love her forever.

"Lana, I need to be heart-whole to offer this woman a diamond ring. I came back to West Central yesterday to face my memories. To bury them. I wanted to be certain that my feelings for you were over."

That little, private piece of her heart died. Emotions flashed through her, one by one. Shame, that she'd even saved a corner of her heart for him. Sorrow, for what had never truly been between them and never would be. Then rage, over the fresh pain he was bringing her.

The rage obliterated everything else. She snatched her portfolio off the window ledge and nearly tipped her chair over as she stood.

"Lana, wait."

She'd made it only one step before Braden grabbed her arm, as she had grabbed his just yesterday by the elevator.

She shook his hand off in a vicious, decisive move. "Do you really expect me to sit here and listen to you break up with me again? My God, Braden, how could you? How *could* you?"

She strode out of the romantic restaurant, letting the fury keep her head high as every person in the place watched her exit.

Braden spotted Lana as she was trying to open the door of an older car, a plain vehicle that was parallel parked on the street. She was illuminated by the glow of the streetlights, her figure highlighted every few seconds by the headlights of a passing car, making her seem all the more vividly alive against a flat black night.

God, she was beautiful. In every flash from the headlights. From every angle, in every mood.

But she'd always been beautiful. It hadn't saved their relationship then; it wasn't going to help him now. He needed answers, and the only woman in the world who could provide them refused to.

"Lana!" He was angry now, truly angry.

She was trying to jam a key in the car door's lock. He hadn't seen anyone do that in a decade, at least.

"Go away," she said, but she dropped her keys onto the pavement. She laid her portfolio on the roof of the car and bent down to retrieve the keys, and that amazing silky black hair of hers fell over her shoulders and face as she half twisted in his direction. "Everything I needed to say, I said six years ago."

I couldn't hear most of it through my own grief.

"Damn it, Lana, talk to me." He tossed his suit coat on top of her car's roof, too, then lifted her by her shoulders out of her crouch, turning her to face him. The dry air of a cool Texas night was all that was between them. God, he wanted to kiss her. It had become a habit, a way to settle all their differences, and he craved it still.

Another car passed, too close.

"We can't stand here and chat, Braden. Yes, we're over. Go live your life with your new fiancée. You have my blessing. Isn't that what you wanted?"

She was beautiful in her anger, alive in his hands, but he was an older man now. Six years of unanswered questions had taught him that communication between the sheets wasn't enough.

"I want to know where we went wrong," he said. "When, exactly—because things were falling apart even before you got pregnant. How did that tie in to it? If you hadn't gotten pregnant, would we have stayed together?"

She went absolutely still.

"If you hadn't miscarried, would you have married me for the sake of the baby? Or did you already hate me enough by then to leave? Was that miscarriage the last straw?"

"I don't want to talk about that with you." She twisted out of his hands and went back to jamming her key in the door.

"What the hell—? I was your fiancé. I would have been the father of that baby. If you don't talk about it with me, who do you talk about it with?"

"No one. That pregnancy is not something I want to remember."

It threw him, how badly that hurt. He'd come here tonight prepared to bare as much of his soul as was necessary to learn how she felt about their past. He'd swallowed enough pride to admit to her the real reason he'd taken the meeting at West Central yesterday, but a man could only take so much. If she wouldn't talk to him, then he'd let her go and he'd deal with it himself.

Like I've been dealing with it for the past six years. Always wondering what if, what if...

His pride hadn't helped him, not when it came to his heart.

"Please, Lana. I'm the one who needs someone to talk to. You are the only one. The only one who even knows about that loss. You may not need to talk to me, but I need to talk to you."

Chapter Eight

The scene unfolded for her as if she were watching someone else's life. There he was, handsome. Humble. Asking for her help to get over an intensely personal experience, the loss of their unborn child.

Please, Lana...

There she was, afraid. Afraid that if they had this talk, things would never be the same. If they relived that time, would they tie everything up neatly and then put those memories away, forever? She wasn't ready to let her last piece of him go; the painful memories were all she'd had of him for six years.

Or maybe, just maybe, she didn't want him to know that the miscarriage had been all her own fault. He would hate her, more than he did already.

Please, Lana...

Braden waited for her answer. She stayed numbly in that surreal state of mind, waiting to see how this scene would unfold, when she was sucked back to reality with a crash. Literally.

An ungodly sound from the street, the impact of metal and mortar, bones and glass, made Lana turn instinctively. Braden's arms were instantly around her, his body shielding her for those critical seconds before silence fell. Lana pushed her way out of his arms to see what had happened.

On the other side of the street from the restaurant, an open-bed pickup truck had crashed right through a storefront. Lana spotted the bodies that must have been thrown from the truck's open bed, sprawled in unnatural positions on the concrete. A few people were frantically making their way out of the store, pushing their way around the ruined truck, climbing through the shattered wall of glass that had been the front of the store only seconds before.

As one, she and Braden began running toward the scene that others were instinctively trying to leave.

"Call nine-one-one," Lana ordered him, barely slowing to check for traffic before crossing the four-lane street. Her first rule in any medical emergency was to call for an ambulance. Her second was to never assume someone else had already called.

"Doing it," Braden answered tersely, cell phone in one hand, his other on the small of her back as they half ran, half walked to the first body that lay facedown on the concrete in front of the store.

She knelt by the prone body, not daring to roll the adult male over. He surely had shattered bones that could puncture vital organs if she moved him. She pressed two fingers on his wrist, but there was no discernible pulse. They'd reached him first because he'd been thrown the farthest from the truck. She pressed a hand to his carotid artery, willing him to have even the faintest pulse, but she could tell from the unnatural flatness of his skull that it had been shattered.

"Deceased." She said it out loud, out of habit, although there was no nursing assistant to make notes.

She started working in a triage mode. That patient was gone; on to the next. Adult female, supine. Lana found a pulse with one hand and opened each eye with her other, looking for any response in the pupil. She had no penlight to flash and had to rely on the store's exterior lighting to produce some response. *Fixed and dilated, no apparent hemorrhage site, pulse regular.*

"Level one," she hollered. "Transport to trauma center." She glanced around to see if any police or paramedics had arrived to take her orders yet. None. There was no one here—except Braden.

Braden, and a growing cluster of shocked, bewildered people.

He stepped away from her, onto a sidewalk that was not covered in shattered glass. "If you need assistance, come here, to the mailbox." He repeated his order, cupping his hands around his mouth as a makeshift megaphone.

It was the most efficient way to approach triage at a large accident site like this. Victims who could follow an order, did. By being able to physically seek help, they weeded themselves out of the pile of more seriously wounded, letting the emergency responders—in this case, that meant her—immediately know they must be lower priority. Those patients needed to be seen, but they wouldn't be dead if they didn't make it to the hospital in the first minutes after the event.

Resources were finite. There was only so much space in a medevac helicopter, only so many ambulances on call tonight. Lana's job was to start deciding who needed the transportation the most. Braden was making her job easier.

The next victim was a conscious male, bleeding profusely through his jeans. Fully aware that she had no gloves to protect her from any blood-borne diseases, she grabbed the patient's own baseball cap out of his jacket pocket and used that as a poor barrier while she palpated his leg and found the laceration.

"Pressure bandage," she ordered, although no one was around to respond. But she'd keep giving verbal orders, because paramedics would be arriving any minute. Braden had made the call.

She glanced around her immediate area, futilely looking for any kind of cloth that wasn't covered in shattered glass, anything she might use to staunch this life-threatening flow of blood.

"Lana."

She looked up to see Braden folding a sweatshirt into a square before passing it to her. She carefully covered the greatest portion of the laceration, then pressed down, hard, with both hands.

"I need to move on," she said.

"Go." Braden's hands replaced hers. As she was moving to the next patient, she heard Braden instructing someone else to take his place. "Push hard, harder than you think you should, and don't let up for any reason until a medic tells you to."

Then he was beside her again, folding a jacket he must have acquired from an onlooker, taking over for Lana and applying the makeshift pressure bandage himself to yet another unconscious male.

"Level one, transport to trauma center," she said automatically, and he nodded as she moved on.

Sirens sounded in the distance, rapidly growing in volume as she made her way to the people in the truck's cab. The one wearing a seat belt looked awful, but the facial lacerations from the flying glass weren't near any major blood vessels, and the woman had no broken bones, thanks to the dashboard airbag.

"Level three," she said, and this time a young man in a blue uniform jogged up next to her and answered "check" as he snapped on a pair of latex gloves.

"I'm Dr. Donnoli from West Central. You have a level one there, the female in the red shirt."

"Check."

"Male with the ball cap on his chest, also level one, but any hospital can handle the laceration."

"Check."

She pointed at the last man that Braden still crouched over. "Level one, unilateral nonreactive pupil, as best as I could tell in this light, and both pupils were trending toward an oval shape. Do you have a medevac?"

"On its way."

"That patient should go by air." Lana looked at the shattered building. "Those were the outside casualties. I'm going inside."

"We've got it. There's already a crew inside."

She glanced at his uniform. Thank God he was a fireman. She could only do so much here as a doctor; firemen were better trained to remove the injured from a wrecked building.

Lana stood by in case she was needed to assist in CPR if one of the suspected head-trauma patients should arrest. The scene quickly became overrun with more than enough emergency personnel as what seemed to be every fire truck and ambulance in the Austin area arrived. Each patient on the pavement had two medics and a stretcher within minutes.

Braden stayed with his patient. She watched him as he kept applying pressure through the folded jacket, never letting up while the paramedics slid a long backboard under the patient, strapping it in place and using it to lift the patient to the stretcher. Braden worked with the team as though he'd done it all his life, jogging alongside the rolling stretcher, keeping the pressure on the injury as they readied a more sterile bandage to take its place. The transfer of applied pressure from Braden's hands to the paramedic's was textbook perfect.

He would have been a great doctor.

As his patient's ambulance pulled away, Braden scanned the area. Lana knew, absolutely, that he was looking for her. Their eyes met, and she gave him the thumbs-up sign.

He nodded and headed over to a policeman. Lana walked toward them, waiting as Braden informed the police that the cluster of people on the sidewalk were the walking wounded, injured but self-ambulatory, able to wait for the second wave of hospital transportation.

Then Braden turned to her. They stood apart—achingly apart—until he said, "Good work, Lana."

"You, too."

As they turned to walk back to their cars, Braden rested his hand on her lower back. She wished she could lean into him as her adrenaline rush subsided and fatigue took its place.

Fatigue and sadness. He should have been a doctor. They should have married, chosen a suburb of Austin and set up a practice. They would have spent a couple of lean years getting established, paying down those monstrous student loans, and then they would have started their family. It would have been an ideal life. It was what she'd envisioned when he'd dropped to one knee in the chapel.

But it hadn't happened, because he hadn't wanted it to. Although he'd taken care of accident victims tonight, she needed to remember that yesterday, he'd stopped the development of a drug that had been working for children. She and Braden had worked well together, once upon a time, and tonight had proven they still could. But she also knew, as she'd known then, that what he wanted to achieve in his life and what she valued in her life were two different things.

Hadn't he reached that conclusion himself? Hadn't he said he was prepared to move on? He'd bought someone else a diamond ring. Braden was ready to propose to another woman—after he talked to Lana tonight.

He was going to marry someone else, and she was going to have to accept that, sooner or later.

She wished it could be later.

"Come here."

Lana let Braden tug her by the hand to stand in the brightest light at the entry to the restaurant. He picked up her other hand, too, and started looking them over like an efficient clinician.

"You didn't have any cuts on your hands before the accident? You didn't get any new cuts from the glass tonight?" His questions were brisk. "We had minimal protection against blood-borne infections."

"You still think like a doctor, you know."

"My career is in medicine. Don't be so surprised."

"Intact skin is still a good defense. I've got no open cuts. Do you?" She switched positions, holding his hands up to the light. "No breaks in the skin that I can see. But we should go inside and wash up."

He held the door open for her and muttered, "This will be fun."

She stopped on the threshold. "We made something of a scene when we walked out. Now look at us. If they didn't hear the crash, they'll think we got into a catfight after we left."

Braden managed to look offended. "Men don't do catfights."

"Then they'll assume we had a boxing match."

"I don't box with women."

Lana burst out laughing at his indignation, and Braden realized she was pulling his leg and started laughing with her. "We're giving everyone something to talk about, at any rate."

The shared laughter was as intimate as any kiss. It wasn't appropriate, really, not when he was seeing another woman, so Lana turned and walked back into the restaurant she'd stormed out of.

In the sanctity of the ladies' room, Lana took her time scrubbing up thoroughly, then lightly reapplied some powder and brushed out her hair. They were going to have the big, final talk tonight and close the book on their history together. She didn't want his last memory of her to be as a tired, wrung-out mess, even if that was how she felt inside.

When her hospital pager vibrated in her purse, she felt as if she'd gotten a stay of execution. She found Braden waiting for her by the bar.

"I need to get to the E.R.," she said. "My pager went off."

"I figured you'd be called in." He nodded toward the bar's TV. "There's a factory fire somewhere on the north side of Austin. I'm guessing West Central is the closest E.R."

She half laughed. "True enough. It isn't west and it isn't central, but it is north. They really got that name wrong, didn't they?"

Her smile faded as she watched his smile fade, too. He remembered.

"You can't be both," he said, completing their old joke.

She was embarrassed to have brought up that memory. "I've got to call for a taxi. I think my car battery is dead. The doors wouldn't unlock and the headlights didn't flash."

"I guessed that, too." He jingled his car keys in one hand. "I was already fixing to drive you to the hospital."

"'Fixing to'? That's the first thing I've heard you say like a Texan all night. You've really lost your accent."

"You think?" His intentional drawl was thicker than his real accent had ever been. "City folk didn't seem to like it."

The bartender came out from a kitchen door and set a white paper bag in front of them. Braden gave him a few bills and told him to keep the change. "Let's go," he said in his normal accent. "My car is cleaner than a taxi."

"You don't have to do that."

He took her elbow and steered her to the door. "You'll get to those patients a lot quicker."

That was true. People needed her. As much as she didn't want to be alone with Braden, the needs of the patients were more important. Braden could get her to the hospital. She followed him to a black sports car parked only a few spaces away from hers.

He opened the passenger-side door. "Have a seat. I'll get our stuff."

She'd completely forgotten about her portfolio and his

suit jacket, the symbols of their business involvement. Both had been left on the roof of her car while they'd had that intense conversation. The one that had ended with *Please, Lana. I'm the one who needs someone to talk to.*

She had no chance to dwell on that. He was back already and sliding behind the wheel.

He set the paper bag on her lap. "Your dinner."

"I didn't order anything before we…you know. Before I left the restaurant."

"I ordered it while you were cleaning up. You're in for a long night. You push yourself too hard without food and sleep, as I recall."

"Oh." The familiar guilt washed over her. She'd pushed herself that way when she was pregnant. No food, no sleep, just hospital work, long hours, weeks without time off…

"That was very thoughtful of you," she said. If he only knew how little she deserved his concern.

There was no point in getting nostalgic about how he'd once forced her to take breaks and eat in the hospital cafeteria with him. They were through, and they'd been through for a long time. Another woman was getting a ring.

Lana was getting a sandwich.

That kind of put it all back into perspective.

Braden drove them swiftly north, toward West Central. The irony didn't escape him. If you couldn't have things both ways, you certainly couldn't have them three ways.

Hell, he wasn't having anything his way right now. The clock was ticking. Claudia was going to arrive in Austin for Valentine's weekend.

She'd undoubtedly guessed—correctly—that he intended to propose. He'd gone to the most current jewelry designer in Manhattan. When none of the symbolic circles of precious metals and unbreakable stones had seemed like something he ought to give Claudia, he'd known it was time to go to Austin. He'd find the right ring after he faced his memories in West Central's chapel.

So much for that plan. Life never happened the way one expected. His "memory" was sitting beside him now, eating her sandwich in silence.

Braden was supposed to be in New York, but instead, he was making sure a woman got something to eat before she spent the next few hours quite possibly saving lives. They'd already worked together tonight, doing just that, partners like they'd once been. Now he was back in his old role as protector, making sure she had food, making sure she had a safe way to get to work. It felt familiar.

It felt right.

The memory that was bothering him, he realized, was not the promise he'd made in a chapel. Neither was it opening his mail and finding a ring. The memory that was keeping him here in Austin, he finally admitted to himself as he stared through the windshield, waiting for a light to turn green, was a much more recent one.

Yesterday morning, as he'd stood in an elevator in his father's hospital, Lana had spoken a single sentence he couldn't forget. *If you don't want what I have to offer, someone else will.*

A primal sense of ownership and a vicious sense of jealousy had roared through him. Of course, she hadn't been talking about herself. Still, his first thought had been that someday, some other man would have her.

He needed to know why he couldn't stand the thought of another man marrying Lana Donnoli. He had twenty-four more hours to find out why Claudia no longer seemed right for him, or he'd be putting himself, his family and Claudia—an innocent bystander—through a very awkward Valentine's weekend.

I'm thinking of Claudia as an innocent bystander?

Last week, he'd been resolved that she would be his life partner, the mother of his future children. Now he was thinking of Claudia as someone who'd accidentally stepped in between Lana and himself and might get hurt.

He needed to talk to Lana, damn it, but they were already pulling into the portico in front of the emergency room.

West Central's emergency department needed Lana. Braden needed her, too. At the moment, Lana couldn't help them both.

He would wait.

Chapter Nine

"I'll wait for you."

Braden's voice made Lana pause with her hand on the car door, one foot already out of the car and on the pavement. "That's not necessary. I could be here for hours."

"I know. I'll wait."

"There's absolutely no need. I can get a ride home. I could be here for eight or ten hours." She'd already said goodbye to him once, choking on her tears on a phone connection to Boston. She didn't need to confirm with him that their relationship had been broken. She didn't want to say goodbye to him ever again. "I don't want you to wait for me."

"If I don't, I may never get a chance to talk to you. Isn't that the truth? This is very important to me."

She heard the subtle note of pleading under his gruff words and hardened herself against it. "I almost forgot. I owe you, right? You need to talk to me before you go marry someone else." She welcomed the fresh rush of anger. "I don't find that a real compelling reason to hang around right now. There are people right through those doors who really need me, Braden. That's where I'm going."

The expression on his face hardened quickly. "I know. I'll wait."

With a disbelieving shake of her head, she quickly stepped the rest of the way out of the car and shut the door. She did not take a breath until she'd passed safely through the sliding glass doors of the ambulance entrance, back to her world.

The emergency room wasn't as swamped as she'd expected. Most of the injuries from the factory fire were minor, so she and the other doctors who'd been called in to supplement the regular E.R. staff were able to turn the beds quickly, working their way steadily through the waiting-room crowd.

Still, by the third hour, her feet were killing her. Sensible pumps had allowed her to jog across a highway, perform triage in a parking lot and stand for hours as she stitched lacerations and explored wounds for debris. But low heeled and well made or not, pumps were pumps. Her toes objected to being squashed into a triangle shape after midnight.

One of the victims from the evening's pickup-truck accident passed her on a gurney, being rolled back into the E.R. from the radiology department and parked in a curtained-off treatment area. Radiology had taken X-rays that showed there was still a shard of glass lodged deep in the patient's arm. While the nurse got the surgical tray ready, Lana stood outside the curtains and surreptitiously stepped out of one pump.

The tile felt cool on the sole of her foot as she wiggled her toes.

"These might go better with that white lab coat."

Braden's voice startled her. She whipped her head around to find him just a few feet away, dangling her pair of white Keds from his hand.

"Where'd you find them?" she asked, too surprised to make a grab for them.

"From your car, of course."

"But—"

"If you want them, come here and get them."

Lana shoved her foot back in her painful pump and followed Braden behind the nurses' station. Without further ado, she stepped out of her pumps and balanced on one foot while pulling the flat canvas shoe on the other.

Braden steadied her with a hand on her elbow. "I went back to see if I could jump-start your dead battery."

"I left my keys in your car?"

"And your portfolio. Your battery was a goner, though, so I had to get you a new one."

She stopped with the second shoe in her hand. "You got me a new car battery? In the middle of the night?"

"They sell them at all the twenty-four-hour mega-center stores. It was no big deal. I'll drive you back to your car after your shift."

"Well—but—that was very nice of you. You'll have to let me pay you back."

He shook off her offer. "It was cheaper than a real meal at Viejo Mundo would have been."

He'd gone to the trouble of fixing her car. For the first time in a very long time, someone had taken care of her.

She swallowed with a suddenly tight throat and finished tying the second shoe. It would do no good to start feeling sorry for herself. It was her choice to be single and to focus on her career. Her choice to live independently.

Like the independent woman she was, she turned to face him, standing squarely on her own two feet, feet that felt a million times better on cushioned, flat soles.

She looked into Braden's eyes, the eyes of the man she'd once loved. The face of the man who had always made her life easier like this, in a million little ways. But the man who had just made sure she had comfortable Keds to work in was also the man who based his decisions on profit.

She should have been shielded from him by her job. "Did they let you walk back here without any kind of hospital ID?"

"Basically. Some of the staff remember us. I told them I needed to bring you your shoes."

And, of course, he'd been waved right on in. He was a MacDowell. She sighed in defeat. "I've got to go. I'll be the third person tonight to pick glass out of this man's arm, poor guy. He's from the truck accident."

Braden matched her somber tone. "Go, then. I'll hold these black shoes until you're done for the day."

"Really, if you'll just leave the keys, I can get a ride back to the restaurant. Thanks for the battery, but I might be here for hours yet. You can leave."

"I'm not going back to New York, Lana. Not until we talk. I'll be waiting somewhere quiet. The chapel."

The chapel was nothing like he remembered. It wasn't the oasis he'd built it up to be in his memory, but consisted of only four walls, a few rows of plain pews and a nondenominational, generic altar that could work for any religion in a pinch.

He'd been sitting here for a little more than an hour,

spending less time thinking about his past and more time thinking about the present-day Lana. He'd spied on her for a short time from the nurses' station. It was good to see her working. She had a way with patients that expressed confidence without being intimidating. After opening the patient's curtain, she'd explained that there was still one last piece of glass that didn't want to be found. "The good news is you've been assigned to me now, because glass fears me." The patient had managed a bit of a smile.

Lana had a gift. He'd always known it. It was why he'd never tried to change her mind about being a doctor, even though marrying a physician meant he'd be marrying a woman who would be away from home countless evenings and weekends and holidays.

She hadn't shown him the same respect. After they'd completed their three-year residency, she'd been offered the honor of a fourth year as chief resident. She'd wanted him to stick around and take an extra year in a surgery or critical-care residency, just to give medicine a chance—as if eight years of college and medical school and three years of residency hadn't been enough for him to know whether it was the right career for him yet.

Then she'd tried to get him to turn down an offer to attend the most prestigious school in the nation, telling him if all he wanted was an MBA, he could just as easily get it at one of the colleges near Austin, while she served her year as chief resident.

If that was all he wanted.

Braden had been certain that a lifetime of happiness with Lana could only happen if he wasn't stuck day after day in the same rut his father had treaded. He'd needed to get off the track he was on. He'd needed to change gears and get his MBA.

To her, an MBA had meant less than an M.D. She'd thought getting an MBA was a step down. That he'd chosen some lame loser career compared to hers.

If she hadn't felt that way, would he have gotten his MBA somewhere in Texas? Somewhere closer to his fiancée? Would they have gotten married as planned?

But he'd felt it, deep down, her disdain for pursuing business instead of medicine. To compensate, he'd gone to Harvard. Not even a doctor could look down her nose at a man with an MBA from Harvard. He'd been competing with his fiancée, going one better than she had.

Braden sat heavily in one of the wooden pews. A painting of sun rays breaking through clouds decorated one wall. *Forgiveness* was the caption on the little plaque beneath it. A day ago, he'd thought he needed to forgive and forget Lana. Now he wasn't so sure. He might need to forgive a younger version of himself for being so vain that he'd assumed a woman would tolerate a two-year separation in order to marry a man destined for corporate success.

Vanity.

He stared at the painting. As long as he was attempting to examine himself, could he admit that vanity stemmed from insecurity? He'd had qualms about marrying someone who would always garner a certain amount of respect by virtue of her career. He'd perhaps thought that an MBA from Harvard meant they'd be marrying as equals, even if he wasn't a physician like she was.

Instead, she'd dumped him. Coldheartedly. No explanation beyond the fact that she wasn't pregnant anymore, so their engagement was off. He'd had no chance to ask why. The injustice of it smoldered, still. Always, a slow burn in the back of his mind.

He was still ruminating on all the ways the future that had begun in this chapel had died when Lana stopped in the doorway.

"I was afraid you'd be here," she said. "Must we really do this? Here?"

He stood and faced her, consciously keeping his facial expression neutral. He tried for a lighter tone. "The odds of us being interrupted by a car wreck here are pretty small."

The joke fell flat. She looked exhausted.

He shoved his fists into his pockets. "Are you okay? That was a hard situation at the accident scene."

She waved off his concern. "I've been a doctor for a while now. I saw much worse in Washington."

He noticed she didn't ask him if he was okay after that ordeal. Why had he expected her to show concern for him? They weren't a couple. Still, she behaved as if he had no feelings.

That's nothing new. She behaved that way after the miscarriage, as if I had no right to want to talk about it.

He'd had feelings, though. And he'd felt real pain when she'd let every call go to voice mail. He'd resorted to paper letters, with old-fashioned postage stamps. The pain had only increased each time he opened his university mailbox and found another one of his letters returned, unopened.

"So, anyway," she began, but then she trailed off in the face of his silence.

Lana no longer wore her white lab coat. She presented quite a picture, standing there in the doorway in her fancy black dress and her white canvas sneakers. She noticed him looking at her shoes and gestured to herself. "You've heard the phrase 'dressy casual'? I'm taking it literally."

He didn't want to say it, but it was too ingrained from their years together. "Is it dressy or is it casual? You can't be both."

She only sighed and smiled a small, sad smile. "So, where did we leave off," she said as she checked her watch, "six hours ago?"

Six hours. She looked tired. Tired and soft and wary. He stepped closer to her and pulled his hands out of his pockets before he realized his intent. She wouldn't appreciate a hug from him, so he let his hands drop to his sides.

"I was asking when you thought our engagement went sour."

Her chin went up. He knew, instantly, that he was going to hear the same kind of thing she'd said in the restaurant. She somehow blamed him, although he had not—he never would have—called off their engagement.

Lana said, "I don't have to think. I know. It went sour when I miscarried, and we were so far apart."

"We were so far apart how? Emotionally or geographically?"

"Don't be silly."

"I'm deadly serious. I missed the signs with you until it was too late. I want to know what I did wrong."

"How can you not know? You moved to Boston, and then you got me pregnant!" She blinked at her own outburst, as surprised as he.

"*I* got *you* pregnant? That's an accusation if I ever heard one."

"Well, you did. You flew in that weekend. I hadn't asked you to come."

"It was supposed to be a surprise. I assure you, I didn't return to get you pregnant. Did you hate the fact that you were pregnant, or did you just hate the fact that I was the father? Had you already decided I wasn't good enough?"

She didn't answer him, but bit her lip and looked toward the altar. He knew what she was seeing, because he'd stared at them for the past hour: bud vases. Two with pink ribbons, one with blue. Three babies had been born in the hospital recently, or at least three babies whose parents had chosen to make an offering of flowers.

He'd never had the chance to leave one of those vases, and the only woman he'd ever shared a pregnancy with was currently shrugging her shoulders and clamming up. He was sick and tired of the way she'd rejected his attempts to talk about it six years ago. Sick that she would reject him again now.

It had been his baby, too, damn it.

"I want to know. Was it all my fault you got pregnant?"

She looked back at him, expression carefully neutral, lips stiff. "I told you earlier that I don't want to talk about it. It will always be my biggest regret."

Being pregnant with his child was her biggest regret?

She'd been so upset when she'd first called him with the news that they were going to be parents. *Oh, God, Braden, I'm pregnant.* He'd wanted to hold her, soothe her, reassure her, but there was little he could do over a telephone line.

The visit where she had gotten pregnant had also been the visit that had wiped out what money he'd saved to fly to Texas. So he'd done his best over the phone to reassure his fiancée that the pregnancy was unplanned, yes, but it wasn't a tragedy.

She hadn't agreed.

I can't be a mother and complete this residency. Not

working as many hours as I do. Not with you in Boston. It will be impossible.

A few more weeks had passed, weeks of missed calls and short text messages: ER full. No break 2nite.

Then she'd finally found the time to call him again, weeks later. More tears. The pregnancy was over, and they were over. No, she didn't want to try again, she didn't want to marry him, the residency was too consuming, it was all too impossible. Then she'd killed all his further attempts at communication, not answering her phone, not reading his letters.

Until he'd walked into that conference room yesterday. Until he'd tricked her into meeting him for dinner tonight.

Now she didn't want to talk about it, because she regretted that pregnancy. What about it, exactly? That it had happened, or that it had ended?

A dark and ugly suspicion rose in him as she avoided looking him in the eye, staring instead at the plush carpet. It had occurred to him before, but he'd always pushed it away. No matter how despairing she'd sounded on the phone, no matter how adamant she'd been that she couldn't juggle a pregnancy and a residency, she wouldn't have made that kind of decision.

"What's done is done," she murmured with her head down. "I don't want to dwell on it."

"'What's done is done'?" he repeated, feeling sick at the possibility. "What exactly did you do, Lana?"

She made a sound, a breath expelled too fast, something close to one of those heart-wrenching sobs he'd heard far away in Boston.

He could manage no more than a rough whisper. "Did you terminate that pregnancy?" He crowded into her personal space, forcing her to look at him.

The crack of her palm against his cheek rang out in the silent chapel. He closed his eyes, welcoming the pain. The relief.

"How could you?" she cried, for the second time that night.

He didn't know.

He didn't know how he could ask these questions of the woman he'd once trusted with his heart. He didn't know how he could still be obsessed with her after all these years, how the mere sight of her still awakened all his senses.

He didn't know how he'd avoided the truth for almost forty-eight hours. From the moment she'd walked into that conference room yesterday, he'd instantly known that he wouldn't be proposing to anyone else, ever. He couldn't deny it any longer.

"I'm sorry," he said. "I'm so sorry," and he opened his eyes to look at the one woman who mattered to him, who had always mattered to him, who would always matter more than any other.

She was completely undone, shaking like a leaf. The hand she'd slapped him with so forcefully was now pressed against her mouth, keeping herself silent as tears streamed down her face.

"Oh, no, Lana, no. I'm sorry, so sorry." He crushed her to him, wanting to protect her from the hurt he'd just caused. He kissed the top of her head and murmured "don't cry" into her hair, over and over, for long, long minutes, until he felt her rest against him, her wet cheek pressed to his shirtfront.

"I'm sorry," he repeated. He'd tell her a thousand times. "You were so unhappy about being pregnant, and then you called and told me you weren't pregnant anymore, and you didn't want to see me anymore. I was devastated, Lana, devastated more than you'll ever know. You wouldn't talk to me."

"Please stop."

"You didn't want to be pregnant, but I didn't think you would have made that choice." He kept her tight against him, wishing he could physically protect her from the emotional hurt in their world. "I'm sorry, Lana, so damned sorry."

"No." She pushed against him, and he reluctantly let her go. "No, I understand why you asked. I was so shocked when I found out I was pregnant."

Her breath hitched before more words rushed out. "I took prenatal vitamins right away, as soon as I knew. I did that much. But I—I didn't change my life. At all. I didn't slow down. I should have told the attending docs that I needed fewer hours or something. I didn't eat right, I didn't sleep very much, and then when the bleeding started..."

Braden's heart broke to watch the torment on her face, but he waited for her to continue. He needed to know what she thought, *how* she thought about this.

"And then when the miscarriage started, it was too late to stop and think about what I should have been doing," she finished in a whisper. She bowed her head and wrapped her arms around herself.

Like she's waiting for me to do what? Pass judgment on her?

"Lana, you can't think you're to blame. You can't. You—you know too much. You're a doctor, for the love of God. You know that an early miscarriage like that can happen to anyone, for a million reasons."

She kept her head down and only nodded.

"You know it, but you still feel like it was your fault, don't you?"

He'd never seen Lana looking so defeated. It was all he could do not to scoop her into his arms. "We both saw women who managed to get pregnant and stay pregnant when they did everything wrong. Extreme malnutrition, chronic substance abuse. Remember the heroin addict who delivered in the E.R.? But then there were perfectly healthy women who miscarried without warning. Remember?"

She shrugged and gave her shoes another nod.

"You know it's usually basic physiology in the first trimester," he said. "The body is actually working correctly, clearing out tissue that wasn't developing properly." The medical science of it sounded awful, though. He fought not to wince at his own words.

"Yes, I know it," she said. "But when you wished you didn't have to deal with something as much as I wished I wasn't pregnant…it was like I had wished a miscarriage upon myself. It was awful."

He understood. The guilt must have been crushing her all these years. It was misplaced guilt, but guilt all the same. He had to touch her.

He cupped her wet face in his hands and tilted her face up so he could see her. He wiped the tears away with his thumbs. "I don't blame you for miscarrying. I truly don't. I wish you didn't blame yourself."

She gave him a halfhearted smile and started to pull away, but he held her there, making her look at him, at nothing but him. "I don't blame you, Lana Donnoli. You shouldn't blame you, either."

"Oh," she said, as she lifted her hands and rested them on top of his wrists. She really did smile then, a hopeful little smile that maybe he spoke the truth, and Braden fell in love with her all over again.

With the beautiful-est girl in the world.

But tonight, in the restaurant, he'd told her that he intended to marry someone else. Which was, unfortunately, also the truth.

Braden didn't blame her.

It wasn't her fault that she'd miscarried when she was only a few weeks pregnant. Scientifically, medically, Lana had always known that was the truth. Personally, she'd always wondered *what if?* What if she'd gotten more rest, eaten more regularly, slept more hours?

Braden was right, of course. A miscarriage in the first few weeks was incredibly common, not a sign that a woman had done anything wrong. Lana knew that, but to hear Braden say it was another thing entirely.

He didn't blame her.

He never had. Standing here, wiping away her tears, Braden was absolving her of guilt. She felt a little lighter. A little relieved.

A little unbalanced.

"You never blamed me?"

"Never."

She was holding his wrists as he cupped her face. And he…he was looking at her intently, until she watched him close his eyes. The expression on his face was one of pain. Pure pain.

He rested his forehead on hers. "Don't tell me you've avoided me because you thought I blamed you. Lana, don't tell me we lost six years over this."

Her heart was pounding. Her mouth was dry. That was regret in his voice. Pain and regret that they'd lost six years.

Braden MacDowell still cares for me.

Chapter Ten

Beyond Braden's shoulder, Lana looked at the muted lights in the chapel's wall sconces. They formed star-shaped bursts through the tears in her eyes.

She closed her eyes, forcing the last tears to fall from her lashes, and felt Braden's thumbs wipe them away. After that, everything looked more clear.

"You were right. We needed to talk," she said. She hadn't realized how much those self-doubts had weighed her down, how much the guilt had oppressed her—not until he'd lifted it away.

She was still holding his wrists. He was still holding her face, and in place of the bitter memories they'd just exorcised, other, better memories were rushing in.

How it felt to have him look at her like this. At only her. How it felt to have him listen to her. Support her. How it felt to have the right to touch him and be touched.

Precious feelings, priceless memories.

But tonight, he'd needed to talk to her because he wanted to move on. *Lana, there's another woman.... It's been six years.... I went to the jeweler to buy her a ring.*

Still, he'd come to West Central yesterday to walk the corridors one more time, just to be sure the feelings that had grown there were truly over before he made a commitment to someone else. Lana felt some twist of satisfaction that at least she hadn't been as easy to leave behind as she'd once feared.

"Is that what you needed to know?" she asked softly, so very aware that she still cared for this man. "Is that what you needed, before you could be heart-whole for someone else?"

"No," he said. "I also needed to know what would happen if I did this."

Still cupping her face, he brought his mouth to hers, hovering over her lips for just a breath, before surrendering to a kiss.

The feel of a man's mouth—of his mouth—was foreign and exotic for one surprising second. Surprisingly warm, surprisingly supple lips pressed against hers. His mouth lifted a fraction of an inch from hers as she breathed *oh,* and then they were mouths together again, questing, nudging open, wanting more. His tongue swept over hers, and her knees buckled with the rush of thoughts and sensations that all clustered together to mean *want.*

Memories crashed in, obliterating doubts, leaving her with basic wants. She wanted the sweep of that tongue again. More of him. More of them.

Her body ruled her brain. Mindlessly, she let go of his wrists to wrap her arms around his chest, a movement in sync with him as his hands left her face to rake their way down her hair, until he pulled her lower body into hard, direct contact with his. Mouths were not enough; she wanted his tongue more, everywhere, to lap her breasts, to caress her belly, to tickle the bends of her knees.

She wanted to feel his skin, the skin she recalled with utter clarity, warm and smooth, with the rock-hard underlying muscles that she could feel now, through his shirt, through her hands. She kept mating with his mouth, tongues sliding, bodies struggling to get closer—

"Well, what do we have here?" boomed a male voice from the doorway.

Lana's eyes flew open and she jumped back from Braden.

The stranger was laughing. He held a Stetson in one hand but gestured with a pink-ribboned bud vase in his other hand. "Be careful, y'all, or you'll end up with one of these."

Lana was mortified at being caught kissing in the chapel, of all places, in the hospital that employed her. Thank goodness she wasn't wearing her white doctor's coat.

Braden wasn't as paralyzed as she was. "Congratulations on your baby girl," he said and shook the man's hand. "We'll give you some privacy."

She let Braden push her gently out of the chapel with a hand on her lower back. His fingertips weren't quite steady. She wasn't the only one whose heart was pounding from passion.

I can't do this. I can't fall under his spell again.

It was how their relationship had fallen apart before. When they hadn't known how to say what needed to be said, they'd let their bodies find the closeness their hearts could not. Great sex had been only a bandage, temporarily covering a schism between them that had been growing too deep. Their values and their goals were too disparate.

She'd known marriage to him would no longer be the equal partnership she'd wanted. She didn't share his fascination with matters of business, and she'd resented being left behind, expected to support his newfound ambition regardless of its impact on her life. Physical passion had only delayed their inevitable parting of ways—but not before leaving her with that devastating pregnancy.

Braden kept his hand on her lower back as they walked quickly through the parking lot in the silent predawn. The temperature was wintery, and neither of them wore a jacket. Fortunately, the physicians' parking lot was a short distance from the building. Braden opened the passenger door of his car for her before their eyes met.

"I want to see you again," Braden said, at the same time Lana blurted out, "We shouldn't get involved again."

Neither of them was ready to hear a third voice call out from a few cars away. "There you are, Braden. I've been worried sick."

Lana turned to see a beautiful blonde woman in smartly casual clothes striding toward them. Her winter vest was trimmed in white fur, and her breath came out in matching white puffs in the cold night air.

"I flew in early to surprise you, but you weren't at your hotel. Thank God the rental-car company has a GPS locator for emergencies, but I had a heart attack when it showed you were at a hospital at this hour of the night, so I rushed right down here, and…now…" Her gaze moved from Lana to Braden to the open car door, then back to Lana again.

"Claudia," Braden said, and Lana knew from the guilt

in his voice and the sinking feeling in her gut that she was looking at the future Mrs. MacDowell. "You weren't supposed to fly in until the weekend."

"Surprise." With a terribly perfect smile, the blonde woman gestured toward Lana and enunciated each word with precise diction. "Who—is—this?"

Lana wondered if Claudia heard Braden's resigned sigh as clearly as she did.

"This is Dr. Lana Donnoli, my...my former fiancée."

"The former fiancée?"

Claudia's smile was brittle and didn't fool Braden for a moment. Nor, he suspected, did it fool Lana.

"The one you'd never bothered to mention until last night?"

Braden felt Lana's back stiffen under his hand. Well, hell, was he supposed to have talked about an old fiancée with a new girlfriend?

"It was a long time ago," he said and knew instantly that both women hated that answer.

"Really?" Claudia asked. "How long?"

Lana answered, to his surprise. "Over six years ago, actually. We haven't seen each other since then, not until yesterday."

"Well, that's nice to know," Claudia said, looking at Lana less suspiciously than she was looking at him.

Understanding dawned on Braden, and he felt insulted. "I haven't been seeing her behind your back."

"You two seem to have been recalling old times." Claudia jerked her chin toward Lana's middle, shocking Braden into thinking she somehow knew about that long-ago pregnancy, until he realized Claudia was pointedly looking at where his hand was resting in the curve of Lana's lower back.

Braden dropped his hand and searched for the right thing to say.

And searched.

Claudia walked right up to the car, so the three of them could have reached out with their arms and had a big, friendly group hug. "You look like you've been crying," she said to Lana, and then suddenly, tears were filling Claudia's big blue eyes, too.

"Claudia," Braden said, guilt tearing at him. "This isn't about you."

"It's not about me? How can it not be about me? We've been exclusive for nine months, and now you're meeting an old flame, and it's not supposed to be about me?"

"It was entirely about you," Lana said firmly. "He has strong feelings for you, and—and he wanted to let me know, before—"

Don't tell Claudia I bought her a ring, because I didn't.

"—because I've just moved back to town, and he knew we'd run into each other every time he visited his family."

Judging by the look on Claudia's face, that wasn't a completely awful explanation. Braden was relieved that Lana hadn't gotten Claudia's hopes up about a ring. Breaking up with Claudia was going to be bad enough; she didn't need to know he'd been on the brink of proposing.

Lana turned to him. "So, I guess this is goodbye and good luck. Thanks for—thanks for fixing my car tonight." She looked at him earnestly. "And things. Thanks for fixing things. It really helped."

She started to walk away, but Braden caught her arm. "Wait. We left your car at the restaurant, remember?"

The slap that followed came from Claudia. A slap

wasn't as loud in the parking lot as it sounded in the chapel. This one hurt his heart less, but it hurt his face a hell of a lot more.

"Jeez, Claudia." He let go of Lana and rubbed his cheekbone.

"At the restaurant? You bastard. We had a gala to attend. You canceled our plans to take your ex to a restaurant?" She whirled on Lana. "You can't have him back. I don't know how you talked him into taking you on a date—"

"Me?" said Lana, clearly indignant.

"—but it won't work. Braden's not the kind of man who'd two-time a woman—"

That was nice of her to say, especially because she'd just accused him of doing that.

"—but you knew that, didn't you? So you came up with some kind of broken-car thing to lure him out here so late at night. Did you suggest dinner at a restaurant while it was being fixed?"

A catfight between two beautiful women was every man's fantasy. The reality, though, sucked. It had been an exhausting night, he was in a hospital parking lot in the cold dark of predawn, and neither of the women had a clue how he felt about her, because he hadn't had a chance to tell either one. Hell, he'd just figured it out himself in the past hour.

Six years and one hour.

Claudia abruptly threw herself against his chest, and the tears in her eyes spilled prettily down her cheeks. "I love you, Braden. I love you, and you love me, and nothing can change that. Nothing. We'll go away this weekend to your mother's ranch, like we planned. Everything will be okay."

Braden knew he'd never said *I love you* to Claudia.

He'd planned on making it part of the speech that went along with the diamond ring.

He'd been a fool, an idiot, to think he would grow to love Claudia, just because he *should*. Just because he was tired of being a bachelor and she was the perfect companion and hostess for an executive like himself. But he didn't love her, and he'd never lied to her. Not until this afternoon, when he'd left Quinn at Zilker Park. He'd called Claudia to cancel their date to some gala at the Met tonight, telling her he wouldn't be returning to New York in time. A business meeting in Austin had come up, he'd said, knowing that business was not what he wanted or needed to discuss with Dr. Lana Donnoli.

Claudia closed what little gap existed between them and pressed a tearful kiss on his mouth, desperate and salty—and, Braden suspected, designed to demonstrate for his ex-fiancée just how ex she was.

Braden didn't want to be cruel, but he stayed impassive as she kissed him, until she kept her lips pressed against his for so long that he thought she was the one being intentionally cruel—to Lana. He gently unlocked her arms from around his neck and put her away from him.

Lana was already halfway across the parking lot, rubbing her arms briskly as she walked, heading toward the hospital, her refuge, the center of her world.

That damned hospital would never need her like he did.

For now, he let her go.

It was past dawn, early morning on Wednesday, by the time Lana hitched a ride from a nurse getting off duty. Her car sat alone in the restaurant's parking lot. Across the street, the wrecked pickup truck was gone, the glass swept away. Plywood was nailed over the gaping hole in the building, like a giant bandage on a nasty wound.

Lana turned back to her car and pressed the unlock button on her key chain. It worked now, of course. Braden was good at fixing things.

"It's okay," she whispered to herself as she opened her car door and tossed her portfolio across the seat.

Her life with Braden was over. Her shoulders were less bowed with guilt over her miscarriage; Braden had fixed that, too, and probably would have years ago, if she'd only let him. But her heart...her heart felt as if it had a hole in it that gaped like the one across the street.

Braden's life with his Claudia was just beginning. He should have a good life. Claudia obviously valued him. She'd care for him, Lana had no doubt, and she'd keep him climbing the ladder of corporate success, too. Braden would go from single and successful to married and even more successful. Good for him. Really.

Her life would go on, too, as a single and successful woman. She'd never been suited for bearing the burdens of a big family, anyway. Caring for patients would not have left her the time or energy that good mothers invested in their children, and Braden had always wanted children. Claudia would undoubtedly produce perfectly beautiful children, and she'd dress them in the latest fashion and stroll with them in Central Park while Braden made multimillion-dollar decisions in a corner office at PLI.

Lana sat in the driver's seat heavily and stirred the scent of him in the air. She could smell a trace of him, clean soap and warm skin. Braden had sat here, starting the car's engine after replacing her battery. He'd probably driven the car around the block, making sure everything was okay.

Myrna apparently didn't want to hear that. "Then he went with three instead of just one, because why?"

"I don't know. You're sure these are from him?" They'd left the chapel only hours ago. Their Tuesday-night dinner had blurred into Wednesday's dawn in the E.R. parking lot. Didn't the man sleep?

Myrna looked at her as though she was terribly impressed. "You mean, there are other men out there who might also send you flowers? I'm going to really enjoy working with you if we get a parade of flowers in here from many, many men. Dr. Montgomery wasn't nearly as interesting, I'll tell you that."

Lana chuckled as she touched the soft petals. She liked Myrna. She needed some friendliness after these crazy first days back at West Central. "Maybe the florist was just getting rid of leftover colors. Red, white and orange is an odd combination."

"Don't you want to know what the colors mean?"

"They're just random." It was significant that they weren't all red roses. Everyone knew that meant *I love you*. Claudia probably received red roses.

"No, no, no. Listen, the red one means 'I love you.' But white means his intentions are honorable. How about that?"

I'll bet Claudia would disagree.

"And the orange means," Myrna said, pausing for dramatic effect, "passion."

Lana's smile faltered.

"Isn't this fun?" Myrna asked.

"Oh, boy." Lana rubbed her eyes with one hand.

"You could read the card, I suppose," Myrna suggested. "If you don't trust my research."

Lana hoped she didn't look as nervous as she felt,

opening the tiny envelope. It said, *Why are you at work? You put in enough hours. Go home.*

Lana laughed. He sounded less like a romantic suitor and more like a nagging spouse. "Sorry, Myrna, but it doesn't say he loves me passionately and honorably."

Or did it? In a roundabout way, his message showed he knew her well and cared about her well-being, probably more than she did. Than she ever had.

That familiar pang of guilt caught her, but she made the conscious effort to push it away. That miscarriage hadn't been preventable. She wasn't to blame. Braden had said so.

"I got called into the E.R. last night, so I'm going to take some books and work from home." She stared glumly at the large computer on the desk, the one she'd used to compile her list of assets for yesterday's meeting with Braden. Had it been yesterday? It seemed eons ago. "Too bad I can't bring that computer home. I can't believe Dr. Montgomery didn't have a laptop instead of a big PC."

Myrna frowned. "I've only been here for a few weeks, but I remember he did have a laptop."

The two looked thoroughly, but there was no laptop in the room. Not in the filing cabinet, the desk drawers or the storage closet. That made up the entire office, so the search didn't take long.

"Maybe it was his personal laptop," Lana said. "I'll call him when he gets back from his vacation." In the meantime, she'd start reviewing the studies currently under way. Even in the modern era, the paperwork outlining study design, methodology, requirements and results were contained in old-fashioned three-ring binders, neatly labeled and lined up on the floor-to-ceiling shelves.

She took the most recent binder for each of the five studies currently under way and staggered for the door.

Myrna beat her to the doorknob with vase in hand. "Give me two of those. I'll walk you to your car. You almost forgot your roses."

Lana wasn't alone this morning after all. She had Myrna.

Braden had Claudia.

Chapter Eleven

"I can't have a civilized conversation before coffee," Claudia said as she fluffed her blond hair, then loosened the sash of the hotel spa's robe. "Wait until room service arrives, hmm?"

It was Wednesday afternoon in the Presidential Suite of the Four Seasons, and Braden did not want to wait for coffee. He'd followed Claudia's rental car here from the E.R. parking lot, and they'd both fallen asleep by seven in the morning. He'd had six hours of sleep. That was enough. The sooner he ended his relationship with Claudia, the sooner he could put his life back on the path it should never have veered from.

Claudia let the robe slip from her shoulders as she sank onto the mattress next to him. Underneath, she wore a stunning creation of interlocking straps, a gown made of satin and designed to please any male with eyes. Braden had eyes. He also had a sore back from sleeping on a couch's pullout bed.

The Presidential Suite was a one-bedroom apartment, and Claudia had feigned sleep in the bedroom when Braden had used the bathroom. He could have slept on the far side of the bed. It was king-sized, so he wouldn't have touched her accidentally in his sleep, but Braden had the feeling Claudia was hoping that she'd be able to use seduction to slip their relationship back to where it had been.

He'd decided the pullout sofa in the suite's living room was the wise man's refuge.

Claudia lay back and nuzzled her cheek into his pillow. He was sitting up, shirtless, but wearing the plaid flannel pants that had been in his suitcase. She gave him a sleepy, sultry smile and reached up to run one finger down his bare chest.

"Claudia, I'm serious. We need to talk."

Her finger barely hesitated. She stretched a little, and the satin straps crisscrossed in daring ways.

"Really, Braden? That's what we need to do?"

Braden picked the robe up from the foot of the mattress and draped it over Claudia's body. "Yes, we need to talk."

The change in her facial expression was alarming because it happened so quickly. One moment, she'd been doing her best purring sex kitten. The next, she looked like a business adversary calculating a counterproposal. Had her sexual desire for him ever been real, or only really fake?

A real fake. *Is it real or is it fake? You can't be both.*

This breakup was going to be a challenge. Braden thought Claudia's feelings for him were as real as they ever got in her life, and she wasn't going down easily. The fact that she'd flown to Texas was proof enough.

The doorbell rang. "Thank God, it's the coffee," she

said, rising from the bed, donning the robe and moving toward the suite's door in one graceful motion. "That pullout sofa is a little embarrassing. Everyone will know we've had a lovers' quarrel."

Hardly. Since the moment Lana had walked away, Claudia had become the master of avoiding any conversation at all. She didn't want their relationship to change, so she wasn't giving Braden a chance to address it. That had to be the reason she'd let him pull out the sofa while she'd feigned sleep. She'd do anything to avoid a fight right now.

Braden gave her the minutes it took to dismiss the waiter and to prepare her sugar-and-cream concoction that Braden found too cloying to drink. She thoughtfully poured him a cup, black, and returned to the bed.

Braden got down to business. "You said last night that you loved me."

Claudia was startled enough to nearly, very nearly, let her white coffee slop over the side of its cup. "My goodness, that's jumping in with both feet."

"I'd like to know what that means to you."

She took a tentative sip, careful not to commit to a full mouthful if she might get burned. "I knew almost immediately I'd met my match when I'd met you. We want the same things out of life." She must have felt the lukewarm quality of her own answer, because she sighed and set down her coffee cup on the—ironically enough—coffee table, which he'd pushed out of the way when he'd pulled out the bed.

She turned to face him, climbing squarely on the mattress and sitting with her legs folded underneath herself as if she were going to pour tea in a Japanese home. "I think dramatic lines like 'you complete me' are best left to the movies. I prefer to be a little less desperately

needy, so I would say 'you complement me.' We fit together. We can go farther and accomplish more together
than we can apart. I'm good for you, and you are good
for me."

Braden had thought the same thing a few days ago.
Then he'd seen Lana and realized how little his heart had
been touched by Claudia. How could it have been, when
it had belonged to Lana all this time? "You're right, and
it is the basis of an excellent partnership, but it isn't love.
I'm truly sorry, Claudia, but I cannot keep seeing you.
You are a beautiful woman, and we've had a good time
together, but I don't—"

"You are worth fighting for, Braden. That's why I'm
here, so listen to me, please. Don't let an old flame from
school make you do something crazy. This sudden infat-
uation is only temporary. You'd be a fool to give me up
for a woman who was quite willing to walk away from
you without a fight last night."

Braden was silent. Score one for Claudia: there was no
guarantee he'd be able to win a second chance with Lana.

"Or was that this morning? I'm losing track of the
time." In a flash of white robe, Claudia was off the mattress and then back again, having retrieved her phone.
She slid her finger over the screen in precise motions.
"Let's go home, darling. Your assistant can't keep covering for you forever. Besides, we've got dinner at the
Indian embassy tomorrow, and I'm wild to see saris instead of Stella McCartney for a change, aren't you?"

Clearly, Claudia thought that refusing to take no for
an answer meant she would get her way. She was doing
a masterful job of pretending she wasn't furious with
him. Braden wanted to give her a quick salute for sheer
brazenness, but this was the end of their relationship
whether Claudia St. James wanted it that way or not.

"My assistant has not been covering for me. I'm perfectly capable of working remotely, indefinitely. I'll be moving to Austin permanently by next year."

For a second time in one conversation, Claudia was startled. "Permanently? But Manhattan is our life. Everything is there."

"Before running into Lana again, I had convinced myself you'd be perfectly happy by my side in Austin. I imagined you as my wife, helping me navigate the Austin high-society scene."

"Is there one?"

Braden almost smiled at her sarcasm, delivered with her perfect face set in a perfectly straight expression. "It's not all cowboys and fringe elements. This is also the seat of the state government. Governor's balls, that sort of thing."

"I see." She gave him a view of her profile as she gazed out the hotel windows to the city on the other side of Lady Bird Lake. "Yes, of course I'd fly in for those events, but we don't have to make this our full-time residence. You've got a jet at your disposal, and PLI's worldwide headquarters have always been in New York."

"I think if we loved each other, we'd want to be together. Yet I'm ready to leave New York, and you will not move to Austin. That tells us a lot, don't you think?"

"There is no reason for you to move to Austin. This is a silly test."

"One which we're failing." He leaned forward and placed his hand on Claudia's knee. "Don't you see? We're only a match at surface level. We don't belong together."

She lifted her chin and narrowed her eyes. "Don't think this old flame of yours will be willing to jump when you say, either. I looked her up. She worked in D.C. She's obviously moving up some career ladders herself. What if she gets an offer she can't refuse? What makes you think she'll turn down her next position to stay in Austin?"

Because she loves Austin. She always dreamed of opening her own family practice here and building relationships with generations of the same families.

The answer came quickly to Braden, but just as quickly, the implications began piling in. Why hadn't that happened? Their engagement had ended, but that shouldn't have stopped Lana from opening a family practice in Austin, the city that had captivated her with its cowboys and hipsters, its creative food and varied music. Instead, she'd moved to D.C., a place she'd never expressed an interest in.

She wasn't even practicing family medicine. Her research positions kept her from caring for patients directly, preventing her from building up relationships with them over time.

That was a loss. Watching her in the E.R. had reminded him just how gifted she was in dealing with patients. He was missing something, because on the surface, it did look as though she was on the fast track to a stellar career as a researcher, not practicing medicine as she'd once idealized.

Braden shoved his hand through his hair tiredly, then drew it down his heavily stubbled face.

"You don't know if she'd kill her career to follow yours, do you?" Claudia practically crowed, thrilled enough with scoring a hit that she dropped her pretense that she wasn't furious with him.

"I do know this. The entire time you and I were together, Claudia, I had fooled myself into thinking I was no longer in love with Lana. I thought I was dating you honestly, but I was lying to myself the entire time. I'm sorry for the pain that will now cause you. Although I won't be attending the embassy event tomorrow, I do need to return to New York. I assume you planned on returning with me in PLI's jet."

She glared at him. "As if I'd fly commercial willingly."

"Please pack quickly. I'm leaving in half an hour."

Lana leaned back in Montgomery's chair, thinking for the hundredth time that it was too big for her. If she wanted a chair that didn't threaten to swallow her whole, she'd have to buy it herself. Her department was out of money.

It was only Thursday afternoon of her first week on the job, and Lana had already determined that she was sunk. Dr. Montgomery had made some terrible decisions. When choosing which studies to undertake, he obviously hadn't done the kind of investigating that he'd once taught her to do.

The hospital needed to participate in the most promising medicines, so the studies would run for their full length, and the department could count on the funds for their budget. Montgomery had agreed to too many studies for start-up companies with no track record, and for medicines that had only weak results in their animal trials. If it were a horse race, he would have bet on all the horses that had never run a race before, and had poor time trials, to boot.

PLI was one of the few companies in West Central's portfolio that had a proven, successful track record. Even so, Dr. Montgomery had chosen their migraine study, when pain studies were notoriously unsuccessful.

Lana's department would be a drain on West Central if any one of the studies under way failed. Not one, but two were failing. One was a treatment for irritable bowel disease, and the other was PLI's pentagab. In both cases, Dr. Montgomery's preliminary analysis had shown the active drugs performing better than the placebos.

They were not.

Lana doubted the man had made an honest math mistake twice. She doubted he'd made it once. Dr. Montgomery had been hiding his failures deliberately, and the stress had probably contributed to his heart attack.

She'd been so honored to be hand chosen as his successor. The reality was, he'd probably hoped she'd be either too ruled by ambition to expose his fraud or too stupid to catch the pattern of his cover-ups. She wasn't sure which picture of herself was the least flattering.

Lana stood up and sent the chair rolling backward with a push. She grabbed a memento, some piece of tasteless golf tchotchke, off a shelf. Montgomery had left a lot of crappy items behind, along with his bad studies. Lana wouldn't put up with any of it. She plunked the cheap plaque with its plastic, glued-on golf ball into the trash can. A stopped clock with a drug's brand-name logo followed. Then another.

"And one more," she said under her breath, pitching the orange plastic square after its compatriots. The man must have loved promotional clocks.

The office door opened as Myrna returned from her third trip of the day to the mail room. Lana started clearing logo mugs off the windowsill.

"Oh, my," Myrna said.

Lana said nothing, finding too much satisfaction in getting rid of Montgomery's garbage.

"I've brought you something that might cheer you up." With a little flourish, Myrna pulled more flowers out from behind her back.

This vase was wide and ceramic and held the large, oval pom-poms of the little blossoms that made up hyacinths.

"I don't suppose you researched these?" Dang it all, Lana knew she sounded hopeful.

Myrna didn't disappoint. "First of all, these aren't cut flowers. You can replant these bulbs outside this spring."

Lana pictured the cement balcony of her second-story apartment. She would let Myrna have these flowers for her home instead.

Myrna looked ten years younger than she had at the beginning of the week. "I wonder what he'll send for Valentine's Day. This is so fun. Are you ready for the meaning?"

"Not really, but go ahead, please."

"The red hyacinth in the middle? It means he wants you to forgive him."

For what? For breaking her heart again? She thought she'd done a decent job of hiding her pain when she'd left him in the parking lot with his Claudia. But earlier, she'd stalked out of the restaurant when Braden had started to tell her he was going to make a promise to a new fiancée, so he'd known that he'd hurt her feelings badly. Lord, it all seemed like weeks ago, not two days.

"But it's surrounded by purple ones," Myrna continued with a tone of voice that suggested she knew a secret, "and guess what they mean?"

"He likes in-your-face, crazy color schemes?"

"It means 'play with me.' He wants you to forgive him and then go out and have some fun. Open the card. I'll bet it's an invitation for a date."

"I doubt that sincerely. He's engaged."

Myrna's smile froze. "No, he isn't."

"Yes. I've met her."

Myrna's eyebrows rose and her mouth formed a shocked "oh."

Feeling awkward, Lana opened the florist's envelope.

Myrna snatched it out of her hand. "That bastard!"

"Myrna!"

But Myrna was already yanking open their office door and letting loose a torrent of fluid, angry Spanish on whomever was in the hallway.

Braden.

He backed up as Myrna swung her open palm at his face, then held up his hands in a placating gesture. "I've had enough of that this week."

"You cheating, two-timing lowlife," Myrna said, switching seamlessly to English. "If I'd known you were engaged, I never would have helped you."

"I'm not engaged. That's part of the message, and I thank you for helping me deliver it to Dr. Donnoli." Braden looked past Myrna to lock his gaze with Lana. He looked so heartbreakingly familiar in the clothes he'd always preferred over scrubs: a button-down shirt, great jeans, leather cowboy boots that were for work, not show. He looked more like the Braden she'd loved than the man in the impeccable business suit on Monday morning.

"You're not engaged?" Lana asked. The woman in the parking lot had clearly staked her claim on Braden. Lana had tortured herself by imagining Braden and the gorgeous blonde together.

"It's nearly five o'clock," Braden said. "Let's go somewhere quiet, and I'll explain."

"Oh, yes," Myrna whispered, placing a hand on her heart. She looked toward Lana expectantly, beaming at her.

"I cannot," Lana said.

Myrna dropped her hand in disappointment.

Braden didn't deflate so easily. He crossed the small room to stand with her, near her desk. "Why not?"

Lana crossed her arms over her chest, deliberately closing herself off. She wished she hadn't removed her blazer, but her cream-colored button-down shirt and pencil skirt would suffice as her armor. "Why are you here? We concluded our business, and we had that personal discussion you requested. You're supposed to be in New York."

"I did return to New York. I delivered Claudia safely to her hometown of choice. Then I packed a fresh suitcase and returned to my hometown of choice. The rumors became official today. PLI will be expanding its operations in the Austin area. The construction should be complete within the year, and I'll move my offices here permanently."

Myrna made a little peep of approval, then started gathering her keys and phone and other personal belongings from her desk. "I think this is my cue to go. You two don't need me as an audience while you work this out. I'll see you tomorrow, Dr. Donnoli."

Then she was gone. Lana was alone with Braden, which felt too intimate. Too exciting.

"May I take you out to dinner?" he asked.

"It's my first week here, and I have too much to catch up on."

"I could help."

"I'm sure the presidents of those other pharmaceutical companies would love to have the president of PLI looking over their data."

"I could hunt down some dinner to go, then, and come feed you brisket while you do the math."

Lana tried not to go weak at the knees. To have a hot and delicious dinner brought to her was as romantic as having her car battery replaced. It was her fantasy, to have a man who loved her and cared for her.

It was so Braden.

She'd felt like the luckiest girl in the world when Braden had loved her. After watching her mother take care of everything, cooking every meal, driving to every school function, making sure everyone had toothpaste and toilet paper, Lana had dreaded the drudgery that came with marriage. As early as her freshman year of high school, Lana had vowed she would not spend her life like her mother. Her mother had dealt with the house's plumbers and electricians, her children's teachers and doctors, her husband's laundry and meals.

Marriage to Braden had promised to be different. They would be equals, both doctors. They would be working together in the same practice. There would never have been an expectation from him that she ought to have cleaned the house and cooked the dinner by the time he came home from work, not when she was coming home from work with him. No, they'd stop after work and get something to eat together. Neither one of them would have to cook, not when there were so many great places to eat in Austin, places that specialized in amazing food like brisket…

"I was going to take you out to Rudy's for brisket, but it's just as easy to get it wrapped up to go," Braden said, tempting her terribly. "You need protein for a night of number crunching."

She dropped her arms and gave up pretending that she had her department under control. She moved to the other side of the desk and flopped in Montgomery's chair. "I already did the math. It sucks. There's a reason Dr. Montgomery left so fast. Your pentagab was the most lucrative study he had under way."

Braden sat on the edge of her desk, sliding a stack of colorful greeting cards a few inches out of his way. "I'm sorry to hear that."

"It may affect West Central's bottom line."

He nodded. "You'll turn it around, but I'm sorry you're starting out in a hole you didn't dig."

There it was again: *Braden MacDowell still cares about me.* She'd been so convinced that he hated her for not being more careful when she was pregnant, it was hard to comprehend that he thought of her as...

As what? Perhaps as a friend from the old days?

He was not her enemy, that much was clear. The hostility she'd felt from him—and which she'd felt toward him—on Monday morning had disappeared completely. She wasn't sure what was in its place.

Whatever it was, Lana couldn't keep her gaze away from his face. She kept drinking in his expression, appreciating that his genuine sympathy was mixed with confidence that she'd be able to handle the issue. They had made such a good team in medical school.

God, she'd missed him so much. He'd been her dream man, until he'd decided the life they'd spent a year planning and dreaming about—together—wasn't what he wanted after all. He'd left her behind on his quest to dominate the world of business.

"Are you happy?" she asked, the words out before she'd really completed the thought.

The lift of his brow was so familiar, it ached. He didn't shrug off her question, though. "I'm working on it. I think moving back to Texas is the right thing for me."

"But getting married is not?"

"Getting married to Claudia is not."

"Did she not want to move to Texas?" Lana's heart was pounding so hard, she was afraid her voice would waver and give away how much she cared about what Braden would say next.

"I didn't ask her to, because I'm not in love with her. She made a point of telling you that we were in love, but that was an act."

"You told me you were going to propose to her."

"I was. She was wonderfully convenient. She looked good on my arm. When we attended events, she always had intelligent things to say. She is charming to all the right people and was generally very pleasant to have around."

Lana did look away from his face then. She couldn't stand to hear him speak well of another woman. She just couldn't. If Braden said Claudia had been pleasantly convenient in bed, Lana would kill him. She picked up a pencil and started rolling it between her fingers.

Braden spoke casually, conversationally, from his seat on the edge of her desk. "When I saw you on Monday, I remembered the way a man should feel when he asks a woman to be his wife. I don't feel that way about Claudia, and I never will."

She matched his offhand tone. "When you saw me on Monday, you instructed me to meet with your underling in the future."

Out of the corner of her eye, she saw him duck his head a little. Score one for her. She wiggled her mouse to wake up her computer, pretending great interest in the spreadsheet that popped up on her monitor.

Braden gave up his perch on the desk to pull a chair around to sit next to her, bringing them more eye-to-eye. "Let me clarify that. When I kissed you in the chapel, I knew that marrying anyone else would be a mistake."

Anyone else.

She set the pencil down on the desk. "What are you saying?" she whispered.

"It's you, Lana. It's always been only you."

"This is—this is—"

Lana plunked her elbows on her desk and dropped her head into her hands. There was no dancing around this issue, no pushing it off for some other day's discussion. Jeez, how could Braden just lay a thing like that on the table? Only days after he'd said the exact opposite over a restaurant table, too.

She pressed her fingers into her forehead. "You're telling me that you kissed me in that chapel and then decided to dump your 'exclusive' girlfriend of nine months? Which, by the way, was an impressive amount of information she was able to get across in just a few sentences with me."

"I told you she was an intelligent asset in social situations."

Lana sank her fingertips more firmly into her temples at the timing of his dry humor. They were speaking casually, but this was deadly serious. "You shouldn't have changed your life for me. That kiss meant nothing. It was a kiss for old times' sake. Nothing more."

Silence reigned for another moment.

Braden broke it. "I'm sorry to hear that. It looks like I'm starting in a hole, but since I dug it myself, it's my job to climb back out of it." He pushed one of the three-ring binders on her desk so that the spine faced him. It was the pentagab binder.

Lana lifted her head. "At least half the hole is mine, and I don't want to touch it. Don't do this, Braden. Let's just leave it as old friends from med school. It's enough to know you don't hate me for the miscarriage."

"Of course I don't. You did nothing wrong." Braden

stood and took a step away from her. Lana told herself that was good. She'd drawn a line, and he'd stepped back the way she'd wanted him to.

He picked up a card from her desk, one of a small pile of cards she'd received in the mail today. Her former coworker in D.C. had forwarded them, thank-you notes written in childish crayon, colorful notes from children who were happy their migraines had gone away. Lana was abruptly reminded that there was a world out there that depended on her for something more than a kiss.

Patients first.

She nodded toward the card in his hand. "Those cards are from patients forty-eight through eighty. Your penta-gab pediatric cohort."

He gave her a look, but it wasn't one of annoyance. It was calculating.

It worried her. She was about to be challenged, but whether in a personal or professional way, she didn't know.

"There is a way to save this study." He placed the card back on its pile. "We could reclassify it as a safety study, keep it going solely to look for long-term safety. If we found out what effect Montgomery was hoping to gain for my mother, then we could keep this trial going while we designed new studies to test for that mystery effect. By the time we established that pentagab worked for the mystery effect, all of our long-term safety studies would already be completed."

Lana tapped the pencil on the corner of her mouth, thinking of the implications, feeling her enthusiasm build on the relief that Braden was addressing a professional issue. "You'd be able to bring the drug to market years earlier. It would save your company millions of dollars, not having to wait for safety results."

Braden tossed the card so that it landed closer to her. "I think most importantly to you, it would give PLI a legitimate reason to keep pentagab available for those kids in D.C."

Lana slapped the pencil on the desk. "It's a win-win for everyone. Maybe even a triple win, because you may discover a cure for the mystery condition in the bargain."

"It's a definite possibility."

"Is it definite, or is it only possible? It can't be both."

Lana smiled as she said it. Heck, she could've kissed Braden for finding a way to save the study. Children would have continued access to their new migraine treatment, and her department wouldn't lose a source of revenue.

Kissing Braden, however, seemed to always have big consequences. Girlfriends got ditched on the eve of their proposals, for example. Or girlfriends got pregnant...

"There's only one problem," Braden said. "My mother won't talk to me about her health. She informs me that I am not her physician."

Lana placed her hand on the binder for the pentagab study. "Technically, I am one of her physicians. She'll have to talk to me when we send out those recall notices. Gathering final side-effect reports at the conclusion of the study is mandatory."

Braden moved closer. "Except we're trying not to recall the medicine."

"Oh. Right."

"You could pull her complete medical records from all her doctors. She must have signed a HIPAA release when she entered the study. There's nothing unethical about the study director requesting records."

She gave him a sideways glance. "But then the president of the company that funds the study can see them, and he happens to be her oldest son. It's a classic dilemma, and the whole reason our family members shouldn't be in the studies."

Our family members sounded too much as if they shared the same family. It wasn't how she'd meant it, of course, but it seemed a little awkward to say, "I meant your family and my family, not our family." She bit back the impulse to clarify it.

If she hadn't miscarried, they would have gotten married. She knew Braden would have insisted, and she would have gone along out of some sense of obligation. If Lana hadn't miscarried, Marion would be her family now.

The old, familiar guilt returned, but Lana found she could shut those thoughts down more quickly now, with Braden standing here. The fact was, she had miscarried. The course of her life was that of a single woman, no children, and there was nothing wrong with devoting herself to this career. Besides, if she'd had that baby, she and Braden couldn't be standing here in her office at midnight, working together. Who would be watching the child?

Maybe Marion.

Marion, who was not her mother-in-law, but who did appear to have some medical condition that was worrying her sons and was being treated illicitly by Dr. Montgomery.

The moment of silence stretched until Braden dropped an ultimatum on her, couched in the nicest terms. "I came here to take you out to dinner. Let's go to Rudy's, pick up brisket for three and head out to the ranch. You are my mother's physician for this study. You can get her to talk to you. A working dinner is more your style, anyway."

"This is about dinner? I asked you not to do this. I don't want to get involved with you again."

"But you want to help those children in D.C."

"And you're forcing me to spend time with you to do it?"

Braden at least had the grace to wince. "I was thinking more of a delicious meal and a chance to make my mother happy. She was delighted to hear you were back in town."

Lana crossed her arms over her chest, assuming the defensive posture she'd been unwise to drop when Myrna had left them alone.

Braden picked up a Crayola masterpiece and brandished it before her. "I'm trying to save pentagab for you."

"For the children."

"For you."

Lana dropped her arms with a sigh and plucked her blazer off the back of her chair.

"You win. Brisket it is."

Chapter Twelve

Lana was a wimp, and she knew it.

She should have put up more of a fight. She shouldn't have been suckered into returning to the River Mack Ranch by the promise of delicious brisket and pain medicine for children.

She shouldn't be spending more time with Braden. Driving through Austin, they still noticed the same kinds of things, still laughed at the same kind of humor. He was easy to be with, exciting to work with, but he would be gone soon. This was one project. One week. For at least another year, his office was in Manhattan, and for the rest of his life, his career was in a billion-dollar industry. He was an executive in demand, as his constantly ringing phone attested. They were only a temporary team, and if she didn't keep reminding herself of that, she was going to be brokenhearted by Monday.

As she silently castigated herself, she reached into the

paper bag on the floorboard of Braden's rented pickup truck. She snitched another bite of brisket. The warm beef, rich with moisture after being slow cooked for hours over smoking wood, tasted like heaven. The food in Austin had always been amazing. She licked her lips as she wiped her fingers on a paper napkin.

"Aren't you going to take care of the driver?" Braden asked.

Lana froze in the middle of wiping her mouth with the napkin. Feed Braden? From her fingertips?

"Aw, c'mon," Braden complained. "You're over there making it look like it's better than sex."

"Very funny." Lana scrambled through the bag of cold coleslaw and totally Texan banana pudding to find a plastic fork. She'd never let the man lick her fingers. Not now.

Now they were business associates.

She fed Braden a bite of brisket with a flimsy fork. He kept the fork in his white teeth for a second too long when she tried to pull it away, taking his eyes from the road just long enough to wink at her. Then he scraped all the good brisket off the fork and into his mouth.

"Almost," he said.

"Almost what?" She was dazzled by his wink, by his mouth, by his smile. The man was too damned handsome.

"Almost better than sex."

Lana turned away to stare stoically through the windshield at the rapidly darkening view of cedar trees. The sensual pleasure she got from the brisket far exceeded any sex she'd had in the past few years, which wasn't saying much for the brisket, actually.

It had taken a few years, but she'd finally dated a perfectly acceptable, attractive man and had decided that there was nothing wrong with two consenting adults enjoying a physical relationship. Except…yeah. She had managed it by getting all clinical inside her brain, acknowledging that this or that felt good, and she was an adult, and they were taking all the appropriate safe-sex measures, and so this was fine.

It had sucked.

Unlike sex with Braden, which on a slow day had been hotter and juicier than—

"May I have some more?" Braden asked, his voice quiet in the truck cab as they left the city lights behind them, heading for the ranch where he'd grown up.

Lana fed him another bite of brisket. She probably didn't remember how to do anything else, anyway.

The white ranch house came into view, its substantial carriage lights glowing in the early-February darkness. Braden relaxed his grip on the steering wheel. He'd managed to get Lana out here. Goal achieved. He was at the River Mack Ranch, and he felt that somehow this was where he needed to be to make the rest of his plan with Lana succeed.

Unfortunately, he hadn't planned the next step. This was as far as he'd gotten in between PLI phone conferences during the flight from New York. He'd go to the hospital, get Lana and bring her out to the ranch. Lana had always loved the ranch. She'd always loved him. Maybe being with him on the ranch would kindle something again.

Sheer dumb luck had put those children's cards on her desk, reminding him of one key piece of leverage: the pentagab study. His conscience didn't bother him. Yes, he'd used patients to make Lana spend more time with him, but PLI could legitimately use the safety data if they found a way to make pentagab viable. His mother held the key, an illness she was trying to hide, and it was up to Lana to make the diagnosis.

Braden trusted her ability absolutely. She was a good doctor. She'd solve this mystery.

It was a definite possibility, at any rate.

He pulled up to the front of the mid-century ranch house, a sprawling one-story constructed of wood and whitewashed local brick. Home. Braden took a moment to be thankful that, in his early thirties, he could still return to his childhood home and still be sure that his mother was there, undoubtedly in the kitchen, probably preparing a pitcher of iced tea. His dad had died of a sudden, severe heart attack too many years ago, a shocking event for them all. He couldn't take his mom for granted.

He glanced over at Lana, whose earlier ecstasy with the brisket had clearly given way to some degree of apprehension. He covered her hand with his own. "It's okay, Lana. Mom always loved you. She's going to hug you, not hurt you."

She turned to him, and the grim look on her face relayed all the enthusiasm of someone facing an executioner's squad. "I broke our engagement. I don't think many mothers appreciate women who do that to their sons. This was a bad idea."

"You're wrong. I was here when you called on Monday night, and Mom did a little eavesdropping. She was thrilled that we were talking again. She jumped to all kinds of conclusions."

"And you let her?" Lana swiftly pulled her hand out from beneath his.

Braden sighed. "No, I assured her that it was strictly business. Let's go eat some brisket and get down to business. Duty calls, Dr. Donnoli."

* * *

Dinner was less awkward than Lana had expected. Marion hadn't been completely surprised at her arrival, since Braden had apparently already told her that Lana was chairing the research department at West Central. The only moment that had seemed off was when Braden was pulling out Lana's chair, and Marion had said, "Where is your suitcase? I thought you were coming for Valentine's weekend?"

Braden had finished pushing her chair in smoothly after only the slightest pause. "I told you, Mom. This is only business."

"Well," she'd said after throwing her son a very motherly glance, "you are welcome anytime at the River Mack Ranch, Lana. Lord knows I've got enough spare rooms around here. The lodge is empty right now, too. Where are you living? Do you need a place?"

Lana had stammered something about the apartment she'd already rented, the brisket had been unwrapped and the corn pudding passed around, and the rest of the meal had gone smoothly.

Jamie was married now and had a baby, Lana learned, and she was unsurprised that Marion loved her new grandmother status. She'd raised three boys in this gigantic ranch house while her husband had undoubtedly spent most of his time in the city at his hospital, so being a grandmother was probably a piece of cake for Marion. Some women were just cut out for motherhood. Lana knew she was not.

When they were engaged, Braden had always talked about having children as though it was a foregone conclusion. He hadn't been alarmed at all by the prospect when she'd called to tell him she was pregnant. Then again, why should he have been? He hadn't been facing morning sickness or the prospect of a rapidly enlarging belly making his daily work awkward. He would have flown in for the birth, she was certain, but he wouldn't have had to push himself back to a residency program while he was still recovering from childbirth.

No one would have thought badly of him for it, either. Paternity leave was a rarity. Fathers weren't expected to care for newborns round the clock; they were expected to bring home the bacon. Her own father had been very satisfied with his life, coming home from work, settling into the armchair he'd paid for in the house he'd paid for, waiting for his wife to bring him the dinner he'd paid for. Lana had been required to help her mother because she was a girl, and it hadn't been hard to see that the boys had it easier in the Donnoli household. They watched car races on TV with Dad while she assembled a lasagna and washed the dishes as it baked.

"Why, no, I haven't heard from Dr. Montgomery in a week, at least," Marion said.

Marion and Braden kept talking as if a silent dinner guest were a normal occurrence. Lana roused herself enough to smile and ask Marion for the coleslaw, but it was Braden's watch that caught her eye when he handed her the Styrofoam container. He was able to bring home the bacon. He could bring home more bacon than she'd know what to do with. He'd been born into an affluent family, the son of a doctor, but he'd taken affluence exponentially further.

She had no aspirations to that kind of wealth. Her career mattered. Her patients mattered—including Marion MacDowell.

She wasn't here to get a complex over incomes. She was here to help Marion MacDowell. She'd be helping PLI in the process, but if they could determine a new use for pentagab, she'd be helping the children who had drawn her pictures with their crayons. Those kids were as close to motherhood as she was likely to get. She wasn't going to let those kids down.

Braden sat back and tossed his spoon into the empty banana-pudding container. "I hate to talk business on a full stomach, but it can't be avoided. Lana is here because we have some questions that need answered, Mom. Montgomery enrolled you in a study that he had no business involving you in."

Oh, no, you don't.

Just because he was the president of a Fortune 100 company, he didn't get to run her house call on this patient.

Braden barreled on. "I know you don't think Jamie and Quinn and I are real doctors, but you have to admit that Lana is, so I want you—"

"Braden." Lana cut him off. She wanted to say, *Braden, you heavy-handed dolt,* but she satisfied herself with just his name. "Marion is my patient, not yours. You need to excuse yourself. I don't break doctor-patient confidentiality rules for anyone. For any reason."

"Go," Marion said to Braden, with a little shooing motion of her hand. "Go give the horses one scoop of oats each."

Braden looked from his mother to Lana with an expression that warred between fierce and incredulous. Incredulous won, followed shortly by laughter. "Okay, I'll go do my chores, but then can I see if Jimmy Waterson wants to play?"

"Jimmy moved to Oklahoma, but his little brother Luke is still around. Now go, because I said so."

Lana smiled at the tone of voice Marion must have used with an elementary-school version of Braden.

"Did you bring your stethoscope?" Marion asked as soon as they were alone.

Lana smiled at the woman she'd always admired. "No, I've reviewed the records, and I'm already certain there's nothing wrong with your heart and lungs."

"Speaking of hearts," Marion said, reaching across the table to take one of Lana's hands, "I can't tell you how good it is to see you at my kitchen table once more."

"Thank you. Thank you so much, but please believe me, Braden and I are only working together because of this study." Lana was truly touched, but she was also an experienced physician, and she'd seen patients like Marion before. Marion was trying to steer the conversation away from her health.

Some patients felt that illness was a sign of personal weakness. Lana had walked into many treatment rooms during her residency only to have the patient sitting on the treatment table assure her that he or she was fine and had no complaints. Generally, a younger and exasperated family member would then start talking, explaining why they'd dragged Grandma or Grandpa to the doctor.

Lana cut to the chase—but not until she reached across the table to hold Marion's other hand in hers. "So tell me, how long have you been in pain?"

Lana left through the kitchen door to find Braden.

He wasn't in the stable, but leaning on the split-rail fence of the paddock adjacent to the barn. Lana had to pick her way across the ground carefully, cursing the heels of her pumps, but grateful for the long sleeves of her blazer. Austin in February reached highs in the sixties during the day, making it seem balmy in comparison to D.C., but once the sun went down, the crisp bite of winter was unmistakable.

A dog barked in the distance. Sound traveled far out in the country, but she must've made very little noise as she gingerly stepped around prickly plants, because Braden didn't turn until she'd nearly reached him.

He tugged the brim of his Stetson in greeting. "Hi, Doc."

"Hi." One syllable was all she could manage around the lump in her throat. Braden the doctor had always turned her head, as handsome as he'd looked when wearing the authority of a white coat and a stethoscope. But good God, Braden the cowboy was hot in a way that appealed to a sexier fantasy. She gestured toward his hat. "Why the...? Where did you...?"

"It was hanging by the door. Old habit—you don't go out to the horses without a hat."

"Oh. Right." She hoped the ghost of a smile about his lips wasn't because he could tell how flustered she was by the side of him that had always turned her on. Did he remember?

He reached out, and she placed her hand in his unquestioningly. He guided her last precarious steps, until she stood against the fence with him, close enough to hear his phone buzz in his pocket.

He ignored it, focusing on her. "Did you learn anything new about my mother?"

His mother. Lana felt stupid, stupid, stupid. It was the second time she'd mistaken his concern for his mother as attraction to her.

"I learned enough. She gave me permission to talk to you."

Braden cleared his throat and kicked the toe of his boot into the dirt by the fence post.

Lana understood.

"She's not in any acute distress," she assured him.

"There's nothing to indicate any kind of terminal condition."

It was doctor-speak for *your mother isn't dying of anything.* Her tone of voice might have said, *don't worry, darling,* but she couldn't help it. He wasn't her darling anything, not anymore, but the old impulse to help him lingered.

Lana gave her fellow doctor the details. "She's never been given a specific diagnosis, probably because she's got a cluster of nonspecific symptoms. The overarching symptom, however, is pain. She can pinpoint when it started, after she had what she called a 'spring head cold' that left her with some muscle weakness. Her pain is chronic, but right now she says it is a two on a ten-point scale."

"How bad has it gotten?"

Lana shivered in the cold night air. "She gave it an eight when Montgomery enrolled her in the pentagab study."

"Perhaps the pentagab helped."

"Perhaps. She presents the clinical picture of post-viral, autoimmune-mediated chronic pain response."

"Like a postherpetic syndrome?"

"Yes, but she never had shingles, or any other kind of rash. I asked."

The beginnings of a smile touched Braden's lips. His mouth was all she could see of him in the ranch's dim outdoor lighting. The Stetson made his eyes unreadable in the night. "Of course you did. You probably thought of it before I did. You're ten times the doctor I would've been."

She tucked her hands under her arms and hunched her shoulders against the cold night air, ignoring his compli-

the motion of her own lips as they formed the conso-
nants and vowels.

"Yeah. They're happy."

Then further words were senseless. This was about
bodies, and breath, and wanting. She tugged Braden
closer with her arm around his neck. He undid the single button of her blazer with a quick motion of one hand,
a hand that then spread over her hip, his palm hot, the
pressure sure. He brought her hips tightly against his,
sliding his hand under her blazer to her lower back, an-
choring her to him with delicious heat.

Lana brought her other arm up to encircle his neck,
but she knocked his hat off first, deliberately. It was a
woman's right to make her cowboy remove his hat.

It tumbled down his back. She never heard it hit the
floor, because Braden's mouth swooped down to cover
hers, and her own moan of agreement filled her ears.

Her thoughts scattered as his tongue invaded, a sensation of taste and texture, her brain unable to string
together words like *man* and *mine*. She pushed closer,
stepping so that one of his legs was between hers, the
denim of his jeans brushing the insides of her ankles,
making her crazy.

Braden leaned back against the wooden door he'd
slammed shut, pulling Lana up his length so that only
her toes touched the ground. She could hardly breathe,
but the kissing seemed more important. And the touching. His hands—oh, their heat, sliding up the back of her
thigh, warming the skin he exposed to the cool barn air
as he slid her skirt higher.

She tried to keep one hand in his thick hair as she
reached for his belt buckle with the other, but those
darned cowboy belt buckles took two hands. She knew
that; it was true every time they made love after they'd

been to the ranch, and it hadn't been that long ago. She shouldn't have forgotten that it took two hands—

It hadn't been that long—

Why *had* it been so very, very long?

He left me. I wasn't enough.

She let go of his buckle and jumped backward as if he were a trap she needed to escape. She backed away one shaky step, bumping into a stall door.

The enormous horse whose stall she'd bumped against stuck his head over the side, pushing her, and she yelped.

Braden was right in front of her, catching her hand, murmuring her name. "Lana, honey. Shh…it's all right."

"No!" She moved away from the horse and from him. "No, it isn't okay. What are we doing here?"

"We're going back to where we left off." With firm hands on her waist, he pulled her squarely to him. "Where we never should have left off. We never should have broken up."

Lana pushed against his chest with two hands, keeping a few inches of space between their bodies. "Yes, we should have. There were good reasons for our engagement to end."

"The miscarriage—"

"We'd already grown apart, Braden, and you knew it. That's why you flew in that weekend, because you knew we were falling apart. We couldn't save it. That pregnancy only delayed the inevitable a few weeks."

"We need to try again. This week has proved we still have something worth saving. That kiss alone proves it."

"That kiss was just chemistry."

"Bull."

She inhaled sharply.

Braden let her go. He bent down to retrieve his hat, then smacked it a few times against his leg to dust it off.

"You might want to fix your hair," he said, pulling the Stetson low on his forehead.

She reached up to feel her hair. "I don't have a brush."

"Oh, well." Braden slid the barn door open, and cold air rushed in. He scooped her into his arms again.

"But your mother! She'll think—"

"She'll be thrilled. She wants you for a daughter-in-law. Grab the door." He carried her outside, then turned around so she could slide the door shut while his arms were full with her.

The door's catch sounded loudly in the night. Braden tucked her more tightly against his chest. "I want you to be her daughter-in-law."

This was too much. They'd struck a truce of sorts in the chapel, and they'd maintained a pleasant balance of work and friendship today, but now that kiss had made a mess of everything.

Lana didn't duck her head under the brim of his hat as he started to cover the long distance to the house. She felt stiff and awkward. "Days ago, you wanted Claudia to be her daughter-in-law. It was a fluke that I happened to walk into that conference room on Monday. What if I'd been in D.C. for one more week? Claudia would be wearing your ring right now. You're changing all your plans on a whim."

Braden kept walking without a stumble on the uneven ground. "I never bought Claudia that ring. I couldn't force myself to, and I knew you were the reason. That's why I went to West Central on Monday."

"You didn't know I'd be there. You were as surprised as I was at that meeting."

The set of his mouth was grim in the starlight. "I knew your memory would be there. After sitting in that chapel, I can tell you that I would have flown to D.C. the next day."

"To end the pentagab study."

"As an excuse to see you." He stopped walking and stood there in the night, looking down at her as he held her in his arms. He pressed a kiss against her mouth, hard and firm. Then he lifted his mouth just far enough to whisper over her lips. "It's you, Lana. It's always been you."

Lana ducked her head under the brim of his hat, rested her cheek against his shoulder and cried.

Chapter Thirteen

Braden carried her the rest of the way to the house in silence. Her tears soaked the collar of his shirt; he dropped kisses on her hair. At the door that led into the kitchen, he let her slide down his body once more. They stood on the flagstone porch for a long time, leaning on one another in silence.

Braden moved first, removing his cowboy hat and placing it on Lana's head. "I love you, Lana Donnoli."

"I love you, too." The words were thick in her throat. She took off the hat and turned it slowly in a circle. She looked up at Braden through lashes that were still wet. "That doesn't mean I'd make a good wife for you."

"Then be a bad wife for me. Just be my wife."

She half laughed at his words and turned the hat in another circle. "That wouldn't be very wise. I'm afraid what we want out of life is too different. The problems we had six years ago haven't gone away."

Marion opened the kitchen door a crack. "Are you two still out here? It's freezing. Come in."

"In a minute." Braden bent to touch his forehead to Lana's. He caressed her cheekbone with his thumb as he chuckled. "She'll never think of me as older than fifteen. I guess once a mother, always a mother."

Lana swallowed. She stilled the motion of his thumb with her hand. "For example, what if your wife didn't want to become a mother? What if she didn't want to have children?"

She felt the movement of his brows against her forehead as they drew into a frown. "Then we could adopt."

It almost sounded like a question, as if he wasn't certain that was the right answer.

It wasn't.

"I'm not afraid of being pregnant or giving birth. I just don't think motherhood is meant for me. I know that makes me sound like a bad woman. It certainly would make me a bad wife for you."

Braden was silent. Their breaths mingled in warm, white puffs in the winter air.

"You were planning on having children with Claudia, weren't you?"

"I couldn't get past an engagement ring with her."

"Be honest. You'd expected to have children with her."

Braden didn't want to answer her, because he pressed his lips together in a hard line and looked away. "Yes, I suppose so."

"That pregnancy panicked me."

"The circumstances were less than ideal."

"It wasn't that simple. I was in a panic, and I learned a few truths about myself. Please, trust me when I tell you that I'm not a good match for you."

"I don't believe that." His mouth was warm against hers, coaxing, provocative.

The hat hit the ground for a second time. Lana pulled him closer for one more taste, one more time.

Except with Braden, there was no such thing as a taste. "Braden," she panted, forcing herself to end the kiss. "Don't you see? This is the point where we always fell into bed, but afterward, nothing changed. Just because we're a good match like this doesn't mean we're a good match for a lifetime."

"Stop saying that. Please."

The gruff *please* tore at her heart. She struggled for clarity, for both of them. "We're great in this moment, but we won't last for the long term. Everything out of bed is too complicated."

He pulled her against his chest again with a sigh. "I won't believe that until I've had a chance to un-complicate things. We need to talk, Lana, until we've sorted through everything that has stood in our way. I want to take the time to do that with you."

His mother turned the porch light off and on, making him look up to the stars as he rolled his eyes at being treated like a teenager. Then his cell phone buzzed in his pocket. He looked at Lana soberly and tucked a strand of hair behind her ear. "You're freezing, and we're going to be interrupted too much here. Let's go inside for now."

Lana swiped at her cheeks and shook her hair behind her. "She'll know I've been crying."

"Maybe she'll assume they were happy tears."

"Don't get her hopes up, Braden."

"It's too late for that, trust me."

"I don't want to cause her any unhappiness, or you, either. Just let me say my goodbyes and go. That would be for the best."

Lana opened the door herself and stepped into the bright kitchen before Braden could try to talk her out of it.

Braden picked up the hat and followed Lana into the kitchen. He kept one eye on the swing of her hair as he hung the hat on the rack by the door. Lana looked over her shoulder at him after only a few seconds, a little nervous movement, checking to see if he was still there.

Oh, yes. He was still there.

He held up his truck keys. "Say your goodbyes to Mom."

But not to me. We're staying together.

The truck cab was silent as they drove the dark country roads that would lead them back to Austin's city lights.

He stole a glance at Lana's profile. He'd never seen her looking so miserable. She thought she was being unemotional—he recognized her doctor's mask—but the cost of hiding her feelings was evident in the taut muscles of her neck and the set of her shoulders.

He wanted to make love to her. He knew he had the power to make her feel happy and content, if only for a little while. She thought that was a cop-out, a way to avoid an argument or duck a disagreement, but there was comfort in making love, and an affirmation of that sense of belonging to another person.

But sex, even sex with someone who loved her wholeheartedly, was not what Lana said she wanted. She was right; their history was complicated. He was good at solving complicated problems. They needed to talk. Braden sought the right words to break the silence of the highway.

Lana spoke first.

"What were you supposed to be doing tonight?"

"I'm doing exactly what I want to be doing tonight." He looked over at her, his exotic Polynesian-Italian goddess, with her hair so black, her skin so smooth. He took in the swell of her breasts against her tailored jacket. "Well, maybe not exactly what I want to be doing, but at least I'm with the person I want to be with."

She didn't smile.

Nope, lovemaking was not what Lana wanted. He'd have to live on tonight's kisses for a while.

"Were you even supposed to be in Texas?" she asked. "Your mother was more surprised to see you than me, I think."

"I was in New York this morning. I told you that." He felt as if there was a minefield he was supposed to be avoiding, but he didn't know where it was, exactly.

"How do you do it? Are you constantly at an airport, waiting for a standby seat?"

"The use of a jet is part of my compensation package." This was a bad time to have a discussion. He couldn't take his eyes from the road to see her reaction. Most women would be impressed. He knew Lana, and she was not like most women—except when it came to cowboys. She was still a sucker for a Stetson and a big belt buckle. He tried to kill the smile that threatened as he remembered tonight's hot-and-heavy encounter in the barn. Chemistry, she'd called it. He'd take it.

"What did you cancel to come to Austin tonight?" Lana asked, sounding like a lawyer ready to destroy an alibi.

His smile died as his brain kicked into a different gear. "A dinner at the Indian embassy. Why do you ask?"

"Claudia was going with you, I assume."

He frowned at the road. The glow of Austin was growing closer, rapidly. This wasn't what he wanted to talk about with Lana. "Claudia is there now. I sent another PLI executive in my place, a new vice president we stole from Pfizer. He's a bachelor, incidentally, with a bright future ahead of him. I asked Claudia to do me the favor of escorting the new guy. She knows who's who and can help him make all the right contacts. I predict Claudia will have hitched her wagon to his star by..." He took one hand from the steering wheel to check his watch. "Right about now. She'll recognize a good thing when she sees it."

Out of the corner of his eye, he saw Lana shaking her head slowly. "I can't imagine that life."

"Since it is Claudia's life and not ours, that's okay." He picked her hand up, needing their chemistry, even if she denied that she did. The skin on the back of her hand was smooth as he kissed it. He brushed her knuckles against his jaw, then settled their joined hands on his thigh. She didn't try to move away. "What's bothering you about where I eat dinner?"

"You need a wife who can attend that sort of event with you. I'm not that woman. I never will be. I plan on spending a few more hours at the hospital after you drop me off tonight. I'm a workaholic."

Her chin lifted, daring him to disagree.

"Okay." Braden said nothing else. It was his favorite negotiating technique. Most people couldn't stand silence. They'd rush to fill it and reveal more about their motivations in the process.

Lana held out longer than most people. Silence reigned for another two miles of empty road, at least. The lights of Austin were clearly visible.

"Okay?" she said. "I just told you I can't be the wife

you need to support you in your career, and all you have to say is okay?"

"I never said I needed a wife to go to the embassy with me. Clearly, I don't even need to go to the embassy myself." He wasn't sure where Lana was going with this line of reasoning, so he let quiet fill the truck cab once more.

Lana was a fast learner. She didn't say a word, either. Damn it. They were minutes from the hospital parking lot, where they'd left the car. He was going to have to lay it on the line.

"Let me take you away, Lana. I want to know everything, and this drive won't cut it. I can't watch your face while I'm watching the road, and I don't want to miss a blink of your lashes. Every detail matters to me."

She withdrew her hand from his and crossed her arms over her chest, giving away how close he was to breaking through her defenses. "I told you at the ranch that I'm not cut out for motherhood. I'm telling you that I will be no benefit to you socially and professionally. What does that leave?"

"That leaves us, marrying for the purely selfish reason that we want to be together."

"But we wouldn't be together."

Finally, they hit a red light. Braden turned to face her. "My office will be in Austin as soon as the building is complete. One year, at the most."

She lifted her eyes to his. He was shocked to see them bright with unshed tears. She'd said something in the restaurant about being far apart, accusing him of putting too much distance between them. *Two years,* she'd said, as if that were an eternity.

"Only one year this time, not two," he said.

Lana dropped her gaze.

He'd guessed right; she didn't want to be apart. Claudia had thought nothing of it, and Braden had taken that as proof that their feelings were shallow. Lana wanted them to be together. He'd do everything he could, then. "We'll see each other frequently. Weekly. A private jet makes that doable."

"When your new office is complete, you'll spend as much time in Austin as you spend in New York now."

"Yes, exactly."

Her hands formed fists. "That's not much time. You don't have a jet because you sit behind your desk in New York every day. You must travel constantly to need a jet."

He didn't travel coast to coast every week the way he had when he'd first started with PLI, but he traveled thousands of miles every year. Thirty thousand. More.

The light turned green, and he was forced to move along with the rest of the traffic.

"It wouldn't even be predictable," Lana whispered. "At least when you left me for Boston, I knew you'd left for good. We didn't have a dime between us, and I knew there would be no more surprise flights in for a weekend. I knew I was on my own when—when things happened." He saw her swipe a tear, a dash of her hand reflected in the window.

In a flash, he recalled the photo on the chapel wall. *Forgiveness.* He'd not asked for it for a very specific failure on his part.

"Hold that thought, Lana. Just hold on for one more second." He barely had the patience to put on his turn signal, to wait for a break in traffic to change lanes. He pulled into the first parking lot he could find. The restaurant was packed. Thursday night in Austin meant a hot restaurant scene, and the parking lot was full of double-parked cars.

Braden stepped on the brakes in the middle of the lane and threw the truck into Park.

He'd startled Lana, who glanced back to see if they were blocking the lane. He didn't give a damn if they were. He unsnapped his seat belt and reached across to hold her shoulders. He wasn't going to speak his words to a windshield. She stared up at him, eyes big, too surprised now to cry.

"You had to handle that miscarriage alone. That will never happen again, I swear to you. I should have borrowed money from my mother. I should have taken a collection door-to-door in the goddamned dorm. I should have sold my car, but I should have gotten on an airplane and come down to be with you."

He kissed her, feeling a little wild in his apology, but it was so long overdue.

She kissed him back. Thank God, she kissed him back.

The blare of car horns brought him back to the reality that he was kissing Lana in the uncomfortable cab of a rental pickup truck, blocking the flow of traffic while they were at it. They shared a quick, sheepish smile.

Braden put the truck back in gear and drove Lana to her office. He considered taking her to her car in the physicians' parking lot, but he knew she'd go bury herself in her office rather than get some sleep. He wouldn't try to stop her. That was Lana, always the most dedicated, the most driven person around. He drove to the main entrance of the hospital.

"I would ask you out for another date, but that won't work." He watched her face carefully. There it was: the slightest frown. Good. She was disappointed. That gave him the confidence to go for broke. "I don't want to start dating again."

"I thought you wanted a second chance."

"To marry you, Lana. Not to date you. We don't need to start over. I want to jump into our life again. I want to learn about all your concerns with geography, and children, and professional obligations. Besides, I've got questions of my own, sweetheart. Why aren't you working in a family practice? I want to hear every detail, how it happened, what you thought, what you disliked badly enough about family medicine that it drove you to a new direction. I want to know if you miss it."

"That would take hours."

"Days."

He saw her hesitate, standing on the edge, thinking of jumping back into a relationship with him.

He gave her a push. "Can you give me this weekend? Valentine's weekend. Just you and me, and a chance to un-complicate things."

She gestured toward the hospital. "Tomorrow is Valentine's Day. It's Friday, and I'm meeting the CEO. If he asks for anything new, I might need to be in my office this weekend."

Braden's cell phone buzzed again, and he impatiently shut it off. His father had always hated the phone. In his era, it had only hung on the kitchen wall, but his father still hadn't been able to escape it. He'd taken Braden and his brothers camping when he needed to leave West Central behind.

"Camping," Braden said, as the pieces fell into place. He nodded toward the hospital. "It's the best way to leave that hospital behind. I'll toss my phone, and you'll leave the office. We each have to pay attention to our jobs tomorrow, but I'll pick you up Saturday morning. It will be a belated Valentine's Day, but it will be a whole weekend camping."

"We'll freeze to death." Something very like anticipation lit her face, despite her objection.

"Not in a tent." He pressed his advantage. "We can take the horses."

"I haven't been on a horse in years." She sounded wistful. He'd taught her how to ride, once upon a time, and she'd taken to it like a duck to water. "I never found the time to even look for a riding stable in D.C."

"You're back in Texas now." He winked at her. "And if it helps me win the girl, I'd like to remind you that I've got horses. Lots of 'em. Let's go camping."

"But we'll talk? The reason we're going is to talk?"

"Under the stars. Around the fire. We'll talk."

Chapter Fourteen

Braden knew how to live on his land. His dad had taught him well, and he and his brothers still made an annual pilgrimage, without fail, to this spot on the bank of the rapid, wide creek that bore the name River Mack. For too many years, that brotherly trip had been Braden's only return to Texas.

He stood by the fire ring and took a moment to look over the land he and his brothers had inherited. It was good to be back—and back for good. Braden knew he would never live so far away again. Boston and New York were in his past; his childhood home was his future.

It was right to bring Lana here. They'd come to talk, and talk they did. As they'd driven one of the ranch's heavy-duty pickup trucks and horse trailers deep into the ranch's two thousand acres, Lana had told him about West Central. Her meeting with the CEO had been point-less. Like Quinn, Lana wasn't impressed. Braden trusted their judgment. He was a shareholder, and more than that, he was a MacDowell. He'd have to look into the situation.

Saddling horses turned out to be like riding a bicycle, which was fortunate, because Braden hadn't saddled a horse in a year and Lana hadn't in six years. They rode in silence for the first little while, and then Lana talked about the serious insult she felt, believing that Montgomery had only hired her to take the fall for his poor decisions. Now that she knew Braden's mother's condition, the odd selection of studies made some sense. From the gastrointestinal study to the one for a rare skin condition, they each represented a medicine aimed at some form of difficult-to-treat pain. Montgomery appeared to have been throwing the entire department behind his attempt to help Marion.

He remained impossible to reach, which meant the cruise Myrna remembered him discussing was still under way. He'd probably taken the missing laptop with him. A confrontation was unavoidable. Lana would have to demand her department's property back.

"If he took a hospital computer on his cruise, perhaps he just took a working vacation," Braden said. He counted the hoofbeats until Lana smiled.

"Is he working, or is he on vacation?" she asked.

"He can't be both. Let's head back to camp."

They set up the tent in the bright February sun, laughing when half of the thing popped up on its own, catching them by surprise. Braden found his commitment to talk continually tested by the utterly sexy picture Lana made in blue jeans and a sheepskin jacket. She kept her hair in a ponytail, tucked under a worn straw cowboy hat from a long-ago summer. She moved in a less refined, more energetic way when she wore boots instead of high heels.

He followed as she collected tinder for their fire, admiring those blue jeans every time she bent to pick up a stick to add to the pile in his arms. He smiled at her childish impulse to toss a twig into the creek to watch it race the rapids.

When he could stand it no longer, he threw the wood to the ground, knocked her hat off and kissed her until she clung to him.

"We're talking," she reminded him, breathless.

"We're talking, we're talking," he muttered, letting go of her slowly so she could regain her balance. He bent down to retrieve her hat, then bent again to pick up the firewood. When he stood and faced her, she knocked his hat off, he chucked the firewood, and they didn't talk some more.

It was rapidly getting darker and colder, but the roaring campfire kept Lana warm. Braden kept her transfixed. She openly watched him as he covered the horses with blankets for the night and shortened their leads. The horses were secured to a highline. Braden tested the rope she'd helped him stretch between two trees earlier in the day. It was secure; they'd done it right the first time.

Actually, he'd done it right. Her role had been a childish one, standing by with the ropes while Braden used tree straps and fashioned a rope pulley and tied all kinds of knots she never used in surgery. He'd had the highline set up and the horses secured in a matter of minutes, all done with an economy of effort that only men who'd been doing that kind of thing since childhood possessed.

If they'd had a child, he or she would be five years old now. Would Braden be demonstrating bowline knots and Alpine loops to a miniature version of himself right now? Or perhaps, a version of herself?

Braden left the horses and began rustling among their gear in the pickup truck. Lana turned her attention to the fire. There was nothing like staring at the smoke and flames of a wood fire to let the mind wander. All she saw were orange flames against a black night. All she thought about was a more realistic outcome, had she and Braden had a child.

Braden would be teaching knots to his child during a weekend when he had visitation rights. It was easy to imagine that she and Braden would have been divorced within five years. She would have been eaten up with resentment, left behind to hire a nanny while she finished her residency and he got his Harvard degree. Or she would have moved to Boston and then New York, trailing her husband and moving from one practice to the next, changing jobs before she'd settled in, wondering when and where Braden would be flying off to next, being the one to run the household by default because he wouldn't be physically present. Either way, she and her child would have both spent more time with the nanny than with Braden.

"Happy belated Valentine's Day," Braden said, handing her a champagne flute as he settled into the low camp chair next to hers.

"This is a nice surprise, thank you." Lukewarm words, but the best she could summon after daydreaming about divorce.

Braden stood the champagne bottle on the ground at their feet. Lana didn't recognize the label. It wasn't sold in any grocery store she'd been to.

"I'm sorry I couldn't be with you yesterday," Braden said.

"Myrna loved the roses. I mean, I did, too, but today has been great, really."

And it really was. As an adult, it didn't matter to her if she celebrated Valentine's Day on the actual date or a day later. What mattered was that she was with Braden, who still loved her and who still wanted her to be his wife.

With the hours she expected to put into her job, she and Braden wouldn't be together at the end of every day, sharing every dinner, every night. But when their schedules did mesh, they could have glorious days like today. She thought she might be able to live contentedly between interludes of pleasure, looking forward to her husband's company on weekends and devoting herself to the hospital most of the time. A marriage like that could possibly work.

But not if they had children. A child would not understand that Daddy couldn't be home on an actual birthday. A child wouldn't be happy if Daddy came home the day *after* a school play. It was just one more reason not to have children.

Would a childless life make Braden happy?

She drank in the masculine beauty of his profile as he poured more champagne for her. She wanted him. She wanted him badly enough to consider a commuter type of marriage, badly enough to accept that he'd be present only when his business allowed it. Marrying an international business tycoon instead of a fellow physician was a different life than she'd envisioned, but because the man was Braden, and because she'd missed him with an ache she couldn't ease for six years, she was willing to compromise. Would he compromise, too, and agree to postpone children indefinitely?

It was the kind of thing they were here to talk about.

She cleared her throat. Braden looked her way expectantly. She chickened out and gave him a weak smile before gulping her bubbly.

The fire popped.

One of the horses shook out his mane.

Lana drank more champagne.

Braden stretched out his legs, crossing one booted ankle over the other. "You're still a natural on a horse. I can't believe you haven't ridden since med school."

"Thanks." She smiled into her flute. She couldn't help it—she loved being good at things. She loved that Braden thought she was. "I'm sure I'll feel muscles I forgot I had tomorrow."

"You'll want to ride again, anyway. You love everything about Texas. You love the ranch life like you love medicine. So, why aren't you practicing it?"

"Practicing…medicine? I am."

"No, you're not, except on the odd day you get called in to cover for the E.R. What happened? You were going to buy into Dr. Forrest's practice. He was close to retirement. He wanted you to replace him. You loved Austin. You loved your patients. It all fit."

"That dream had to have you in it to make it work." She didn't want to feel the bitterness again. She needed to explain it without getting emotional. "It was all so beautifully balanced in my mind. The two of us, sharing one practice, one life, one home. And then—"

No, she couldn't do it. She was bitter. He, not she, had killed that dream. The fire was the only safe place to focus her eyes. She couldn't look at Braden, although she could feel him looking at her.

"And then," Braden said, picking up her story, "I told you I needed an MBA, and I went to a school clear across the country to get it. I want you to know that I realize my move to Boston was rooted in immaturity."

Curiosity began to edge out bitterness. The flames danced lower, running out of fuel as the evening went on. "I don't think I've ever heard 'choosing a Harvard education' described as an immature move."

"Insecure, then. You were going to have a career that carried great esteem. Always, my wife would have the title 'doctor' and all the respect that entails. You disapproved of practically every other career, but I thought even an M.D. could be proud to introduce her husband from Harvard."

"Was I really so snooty about it?"

He didn't answer her, but she felt the truth of it. She'd disdained his ambition as nothing more than the greedy pursuit of dollars.

She didn't want to watch the fire any longer, so she tilted her head back to look at the clear, clear stars in the country sky.

"I could have gotten an excellent MBA from UT in Austin," Braden said, and she knew the bitterness in his voice was directed at himself. "Baylor. Rice. They are within driving distance to Austin. But it had to be Harvard. I was too busy competing with you when I should have been loving you."

Ah, competition. They really were a perfect match, even in their flaws.

"Did you know I got board certified in family medicine?" she asked.

"No." Braden stood and started banking the remains of the fire. "That's good. You finished what you started."

Lana stopped staring at the stars. Braden was so much more spectacular, lit by the remains of the fire against the inky black of night.

"I knew you were with PLI," she confessed quietly.

Braden went very still.

"Even though I was board certified in family practice, I was the first one to apply when that research position opened in D.C. Maybe I'd been keeping tabs on PLI's research activities."

Braden stabbed at the last smoldering ember, then turned to face her. "Lana…"

She rushed on, needing to complete her thought. "Maybe I wanted to share the same field with you. Or maybe it was more immature than that. If family practice wasn't good enough for you, then it wasn't good enough for me anymore, either. Maybe I'm in research because I was competing with you, too."

"We're idiots." He crouched in front of her chair and took her hands in his.

"Idiots circling around each other for six years."

"Damned stubborn."

"Too proud."

Braden stood and pulled her out of her chair. "Let's go to bed."

Chapter Fifteen

Outside, it was peaceful along the banks of the River Mack. Clear skies, bright stars. The tethered horses blew softly now and then in the crisp night air.

Inside the small tent, Lana felt electric anticipation. The low nylon walls were illuminated by the soft light of a yellow lantern that hung from a loop overhead. She was zipped up in her sleeping bag, parallel to Braden's, grateful for the thin foam of the bedroll underneath her. A portable space heater was humming to fend off the February chill.

Braden had courteously given her first access to the tent to get ready for bed, something she'd had to accomplish on her hands and knees, because the tent was not big enough to stand in. Now, cozy in a loose-fitting T-shirt and panties, she wasn't about to leave the warmth of her winter-rated sleeping bag to go back outside. Braden would just have to change in front of her.

Braden ducked into the tent and zipped the door shut for the night. Sitting on his sleeping bag, he pulled his shirt off with his back angled toward her. That was fine with her. He had a gorgeous back, all shoulder muscle and tapered waist. Lana held very still, waiting for more.

Over his shoulder, Braden said, "You can turn away."

"Okay."

After a moment, Braden sighed. "You're watching, aren't you?"

"I can be damned stubborn." She put her hand over her mouth so that she wouldn't ruin her tough-girl words with a nervous giggle.

Braden slid his leather belt out of its loops, undid his button fly and hooked his thumbs in his waistband.

Lana held her breath.

With a buck of his hips, he shucked off his jeans, underwear and all.

Good God.

She'd sat across from him in the conference room on Monday and had thought he looked good in a suit and tie. She'd smugly remembered what he looked like without them, too: warm skin over hard muscle. But her memories had been nothing, merely faded glory compared to the strength beside her now. With his back to her, she could admire so much, from the indentation at his hip to the cleft of his backside to the muscles of his thigh.

He flipped the sleeping bag over himself, hiding most of his body from her view as he lay on his side, facing her.

"But…" she protested.

He raised one eyebrow, in what she'd always thought of as the imperial MacDowell look.

She rose on one elbow and pulled her ponytail holder from her hair. His brows drew together in concentration as he followed the movement of her hair, watching intently as she scooped it all over one shoulder.

Gotcha. He'd always had a thing for her hair.

His eyelids half closed in a heavy, slow move, but then he grabbed a pair of flannel pants from their pile of gear and pulled them on under his sleeping bag. Then he calmly lay on his back and scrunched his jacket under his neck in lieu of a pillow, looking as if he were ready to sleep. Alone.

That gave her a moment of uncertainty. After their campfire talk, she was certain they were back in a relationship. A relationship with Braden had benefits—benefits she'd just seen in the glow of the lantern.

Maybe he was waiting for a sign from her. She hadn't flirted with a man in an eternity. She hoped it was like riding a bicycle—or saddling a horse.

She toyed with her hair again, attracting Braden's attention immediately. "Aren't you going to kiss me good-night?"

His gaze left her hair to settle on her mouth. "No."

Surprised, she tossed her hair back. "But you kissed me when we were gathering firewood."

"We were fully dressed. In the daylight. By an icy cold creek."

It was cute of him to act as if she was irresistible. Flirting was fun. "The creek is still out there if you need it after you kiss me good-night. I trust you."

"You shouldn't." He half rose and turned toward her again. The muscles in his supporting arm were sharply defined. "I'm not a teenager, and we're not casually dating. There are no good-night kisses on the doorstep anymore. We came here to talk, but I'm thirty-four years old, and I'm in love with you. If I touch you tonight, I'm going to make sure you beg for more."

Lana's heart skittered to a stop. He wasn't playing.

When her heart resumed its rhythm, it was faster. Stronger. If he touched her, it would lead to more. That sounded more like a promise than a threat.

This time, she acted before she could chicken out. She lay back, arching a little as if she were stretching on a luxurious mattress, tucking one arm behind her head. Slowly, she extended her other arm toward him. "Then would you check my wrist? I think I pulled a muscle in my forearm holding the reins today."

Without breaking eye contact, he sat up the rest of the way. The sleeping bag bunched in his lap. Looming over her, he took her hand in one of his. With his other hand, he began squeezing her flesh firmly, working from her wrist to her elbow.

Slowly, she raised her knee, nudging aside the unzipped flap of her sleeping bag to expose one bare leg. "I may have twisted my ankle a bit."

Solemnly, Braden placed his warm hand above her knee. Watching the path he created, he ran his hand down her leg, until he palmed the instep of her foot. He reverently placed a kiss on her ankle, then ran his hand back up her leg, past her knee, firmly up the inside of her thigh. He watched her face as he cupped her through her underwear for a moment, holding his hand still just long enough to transfer the heat of his palm to her body. Then his hand continued its journey upward until it rested on her belly.

The intensity in his face made Lana suck in a shaky breath. She wouldn't be flirting with him anymore this evening. This night, this sharing of bodies with Braden, was going to be a Big Deal. She had no doubt that she would remember this weekend, forever. She hoped she was ready.

She lifted the top layer of her sleeping bag in invitation. "Sleep with me, Braden."

He kissed her full on the mouth, tenderly, and moved next to her, laying himself beside her, overwhelming her senses as his body touched hers all at once, from her shoulders to the tips of her toes. He took his time covering them both with the quilted cloth of the sleeping bag, giving her a chance to shiver past the first sensation and settle into him. Propped on one elbow over her, he smoothed her hair back, carefully, toward the edge of the pillow. He slid the strands out of the way so he wouldn't catch them and pull her long hair by accident.

She knew that was what he was thinking while he smoothed her hair. She remembered it from before, when they'd been so in love. She closed her eyes, unwilling to cry at this moment. They were still so in love.

"Lana, look at me."

She did, melting with emotion, dying from anticipation.

"What we're about to do might have obvious consequences," he said in a voice husky and deep. "Are you on any birth control?"

A cold trickle of reality penetrated the pleasant barrage of sensation that his warm skin was causing.

"N-no." She wasn't protected, but she didn't want him to stop tonight. She wanted his body and all the pleasure it would bring—but she'd forgotten such a basic thing.

Her disappointment must have shown on her face, because Braden touched her lips with a finger. "Don't worry. There are condoms in the first aid kit. Nothing is one hundred percent effective, though. Especially not condoms."

Her body was adjusting to the sensation of being next to his, freeing her mind to concentrate on his words—

which must be important, because the man was waiting for her to say something when he should be touching her.

"It will be fine," she said.

"The last time we made love, the very last time, the odds caught up with us. You told me it sent you into a panic. You told me this week that you can't handle the idea of having children. I need to know, Lana, before we do this. Are you going to be okay if you get pregnant tonight?"

"What?" She ought to feel as if that icy creek water had been dumped on her, but his body was against hers, too warm to let her freeze. "Why would you ask me that now?"

"Because I can't do you harm. How can I take pleasure in this when there's a chance that it will result in something that terrifies you? It's like playing roulette with your happiness. I can't do it."

She gaped at him, speechless. He was half-nude in her sleeping bag. She could feel the heat and hardness of his length against her thigh; the flannel of his pants hid nothing. He didn't feel like a man who couldn't; he most certainly *could.* Right now.

"The other night, on the porch, you said you weren't able to handle being a mother. Tell me why."

"You want to talk?" she asked, incredulous. "This is a terrible time to talk."

"No, it isn't. We have the entire night. You can tell me anything, and I'll stay right here and listen, and keep you warm and safe."

He'd listen, but he wouldn't like what he'd hear. She wasn't normal, a woman who happily anticipated centering her life on the needs of a child. He'd be turned off if he knew how much she dreaded the idea.

"I thought we were going to have sex." She sounded

like a sullen child, even to her own ears. "That's all I wanted to do."

Braden rolled onto his back with a hiss, a short sound of air through his teeth. He sounded frustrated—or furious. Startled, Lana looked over at his profile.

"That's a damned selfish thing for you to say, Lana. I'm not here to have my heart broken again. I won't make love to you this weekend and then have you decide we shouldn't be together."

I'm not here to have my heart broken again.

With those words, he blew away the last of her lingering resentment for the loneliness she'd survived. Humbled, she sought his hand under the covers and interlocked her fingers with his. "I'm sorry. I forget sometimes that I wasn't the only one in pain for the past six years."

He closed his eyes and squeezed her hand. "The pregnancy was traumatic for you. Take me back there. It was October, and you were four months into your year as chief resident. I imagine you were in your apartment, standing at a bathroom sink, holding a pregnancy test in your hand. You read the result. What was your first thought?"

"That my life was over," she whispered. "Everything I'd accomplished, gone in an instant."

Braden waited.

"I did the math in my head. I wouldn't make the full twelve months of the residency year. I held that stick, and I thought 'all gone.' I'd already lost you—or at least, I'd already lost any chance of the future we'd planned, owning a practice together. And now I was going to lose what I had left. I wasn't going to be able to finish my residency."

He rolled to face her again, keeping their joined hands between their chests.

"I'd deliver near the end of May. You would still be at Harvard, taking finals, probably leaving for a summer internship in some Fortune 500 company in Chicago or L.A., living your businessman's dream, but my dream was over. I'd be forced to take maternity leave at my parents' house, so my mom could help me change diapers around the clock while I healed from…"

She swallowed and barreled on. They'd delivered babies as residents. "While I healed from the delivery. My dad would be so disappointed."

Braden shifted so that her head was on his bare shoulder. "Your dad might have been happy to have a grandchild. He's a very traditional guy. You make it sound like you would have been a disgraced teenager from his era, kicked out of school, but you were twenty-seven, and you would have been married."

"Married to an out-of-town husband, spending my days cooking and cleaning and caring for a baby, like every other woman my dad has ever known. I wouldn't be special after all. When you've always been praised for being the best, being normal can be a failure. Dad took such pride in me being the best."

"Instead of being the best doctor, you would have been the best mother."

"That's the problem. I don't want to be the best mother." She could feel her own temper rising. Braden didn't understand. Even at the time, he'd treated the pregnancy as if it was no big inconvenience. Tonight, he wanted to hear the whole ugly truth of her feelings? Fine, then.

She untangled herself from their cozy cuddle and swiftly sat up, turning on him so he could see her face. "*I don't want to be the best mother. I had the best mother.*

My mom was the best, and do you know what that made her? *Tired.* That's what cooking and cleaning and caring for your husband and your children gets you.

"I learned that lesson when I was young. Because I was a girl, I was expected to be her helper. Every once in a while, I'd catch her standing at the kitchen sink and looking out the window. Her only view was the house next door, where another mother lived, another tired woman. Then my mother would sigh, and her little break was over, and she'd start scrubbing another pot, cleaning it just to get it dirty again for another meal. I felt sorry for her."

She'd started to cry, tears trailing down her cheeks, but she wasn't sad. She was angry.

Braden sat up, shoving aside the sleeping bag, but she held him off with a stiff arm when he would have pulled her close.

"I learned how to wax a floor and clean a tub. I helped the best mother in the world with the dishes every single day. My brothers took out the trash. That's a manly chore. Do you know how long that takes? Five minutes, once a week." She swiped at her tears. "I wondered why they got such easy jobs. Were they better than I was? The answer was obvious, even to a child. They were boys. They didn't have to learn how to be a mother.

"But then, there was school. Everyone got their report cards on the same day. Dad looked them all over at the same time. Mine was the best. I could beat all the boys at school."

Braden bent one knee and rested his arm on it, settling in for her story. He didn't interrupt. He didn't sigh in sympathy, or nod in agreement, or shake his head in disgust.

He did hold her hand, and he waited.

"One glorious day when I was in high school, my middle brother—Antonio, you remember him—asked me when I was going to finish the laundry. He had a debate coming up for the end of the school year, and he needed a dress shirt to be pressed. I was in the middle of studying for final exams. I remember it, clear as day, even the page in my precalculus book. I was taking the same course as a sophomore that my brother Roberto had taken as a junior."

She paused to dash her cheek against her sleeve and laughed ruefully at her own words. "Do you see how proud I was of that? It's been twenty years, and I still remember it.

"Anyway, Antonio asked when the laundry would be done, and my dad hollered from his TV chair, 'Leave Lana alone. She doesn't have to do your ironing. She's got a math test to ace.'

"I'd just been handed the golden key. I had a way out. I didn't have to do all the boring things that my mother did, not as long as I was the star student. You know the rest. I was valedictorian. I won scholarships. I went to medical school. My life was a lot better than my mother's, as long as I was better than everyone else in school." She paused, relieved that no more tears had fallen.

Braden squeezed her hand. "I don't think that was your only reason to excel, but I can see that it added incentive. Your personality is to master whatever task is at hand. I've always admired that."

"It annoys you. Just this week, you said something about me working late because I wanted to prove I was the best."

"It challenged me. You weren't giving up on pentagab. It's been too long since I've had you around to keep me on my toes. I like that drive."

"It's not a good trait. I was still being the best when I got pregnant. I was the best damned resident at West Central, so good that they were paying me double to stay an extra year and train all the other residents. I was pretty proud of myself, remember?"

"You had a right to be. Chief resident is an honor."

"Stop being so nice about it."

Damn it, she could feel the tears welling up again. She let go of his hand and held hers up in a gesture that imitated holding a small, plastic stick.

"When I held that pregnancy test in my hand, I thought how disappointed the faculty would be in me. Instead of chief resident, I was just going to be the pregnant girl who couldn't fulfill her commitment. My dad, the faculty, myself—all disappointed. Do you see how bad I am? A normal woman would be happy that she and her fiancé were having a baby. Not me."

She was sick of her own tears. She hated to relive the misery. She grabbed the shirt she'd worn earlier and used it to dry her face, making an attempt to laugh off her distress. "At the time, I was in the middle of a serious pity party. I'm reenacting it for you."

Braden didn't smile.

There's nothing amusing about finding out you almost married a drama queen.

Lana tossed the wet shirt into a corner of the tent and attempted a calming breath. "I would've had to take May and June off, at a minimum, and I was worried that the third-year residents would take all the openings for private practices in Austin. If I had a C-section, August would be off the table, too. Honestly, I was scared at the idea of taking any break at all, because what if I loved maternity leave? What if I didn't want to leave my baby and start a new job?"

It was as overwhelming now as it had seemed then.

"Can you imagine the irony? I resented being pregnant for taking away my dream of being chief resident, but it was possible that the opposite could happen. After twelve years of effort to become a doctor, I might resent my career, for taking me away from my baby."

Her last words hung in the silent, cool air of the tent.

"Your baby," Braden said. He scrubbed his hands over his face, a move of frustration. "Not our baby."

"I didn't mean it that way. Of course it was our—"

"That wasn't a criticism of you. It's on me. I couldn't have been more absent. Look at all the ramifications you just laid out. I never considered half of them. Would my wife need extra help after a C-section? I never thought about it."

He seemed upset. She knew him, and she knew that when Braden was upset, he found release in action. He couldn't walk anywhere, though. It was cold outside, and they were half-dressed in a heated tent in the middle of two thousand acres, and there was nowhere for him to go, nothing for him to do.

Lana tried to soothe him. "You didn't have to think of those things. We never got to that point."

He reached up to lower the lantern's light. They'd been in the tent long enough for their eyes to adjust, and they didn't need the bright light to see clearly.

"You thought of them," Braden said. "I should have, too, instead of saying patronizing things like 'it's unexpected, but it's going to be okay.' No wonder you mailed my ring back."

"What did you say?" Her words came out as a whisper.

"No wonder you mailed my ring back. It was the right thing for you to do."

She could not mistake his meaning: he was no longer angry with her for breaking their engagement. She'd already learned this week that he had never blamed her for the miscarriage. That left…

Nothing. Nothing but a clean slate between them.

"Braden." She rose on her knees, nearly knocking him over in her eagerness as she took his face in both of her hands. "Braden MacDowell, I've missed you every single day since I put that box in the mail. I hate living without you. May I have my ring back?"

Chapter Sixteen

"Stay right there."

Braden dropped the briefest of kisses on her mouth, then rolled to his hands and knees and started unzipping the tent's door.

Lana dove for the safety of her sleeping bag as the cold air rushed in and Braden rushed out. She listened to his footsteps. He wore only the flannel plaid bottoms on a winter's night, running to the pickup truck. She heard the horses as they let him know he was crazy by stamping their feet and shaking their leads. The truck door slammed shut, and a moment later, Braden practically dove through the tent door.

"It's frigging cold out there."

"Get under the blanket." For the second time that night, she lifted the flap of the sleeping bag.

Braden didn't hesitate to join her. His bare chest was like ice.

"Eek! Don't touch me."

Braden started backing out of the sleeping bag.

"No, stay. You're cold. Just don't touch me." It was a ridiculous idea, of course, because the sleeping bag was a single. They laughed and shivered and scooted around, making room for each other. "Are the horses okay? Do we need to trailer them?"

Braden tapped her nose. "They're fine, and you're a good cowgirl for asking. They've got their own coats, plus blankets, too. It's only freezing if you're a naked man."

"Hmm. I don't actually see a naked man anywhere."

"Let a guy warm up before you make him take off his pants. Speaking of cowgirls, do you want to live in Texas after we're married? I don't want to assume anything."

"Oh, yes. Do you?"

They were cozied in the sleeping bag up to their necks now. Braden nodded. "I can't move immediately, but I'll be home often this year. Way more often than when I was in Boston."

"Because now you're filthy rich."

"Yeah, I kind of am."

Braden's body heat had quickly chased away the cold. Lana was already growing too warm. She wiggled one shoulder and arm out from under the covers.

"You don't like the idea of marrying a rich man?"

She didn't ask how he'd guessed. They seemed to be so very in tune with each other. "It complicates things. No medical practice is going to generate the kind of income that your job does. If PLI needs you to move, I'll have to give up my job and start over somewhere else."

Their faces were close together, sharing her pillow. Braden kissed the corner of her mouth. "It's not a competition. I'm not competing with my wife ever again. If we want to live in Texas, then we'll live in Texas."

"You didn't let me finish. I'll have to give up my job and move with you, because I'm not going to live without you." She threaded her fingers through his hair and kissed him hard. "I missed you so terribly. Now that you're back, it's going to be hard to let you go for even a short business trip. I want my ring back, something to show the world that you're mine while you're gone."

"I couldn't sell that ring." Braden smiled at her, but Lana thought there was a trace of sadness behind his smile.

"But it isn't quite the same anymore. We've gained a lot of experience the hard way, but that experience is precious. Your ring is more precious now, too."

He rose and positioned himself so he was kneeling in the traditional pose of a man who proposed. Lana could only stand on her knees in the low tent. He was bare-chested and she was bare-legged as they faced each other on their knees, but that seemed perfect to her, perfect in every way.

Braden must have been holding the velvet box in his hand the entire time, because he simply turned his palm up to reveal it. "I hope you're not disappointed. I had it altered yesterday."

He opened the little box. The ring inside looked nothing like the simple solitaire she remembered. The diamond in the center was surrounded by two more circles of diamonds. There were so many stones with so many facets, the ring sparkled even in the low glow of the camp lantern. In the Texas sun, it would burst with light.

Lana fell from her knees to land on the floor with a thud. "My goodness. My gosh."

Braden sat beside her quickly. "It's too much, isn't

it? But look, the center is your diamond, the original stone. It's still there, still just as strong as our feelings for each other."

He stopped himself abruptly, then continued with a dip of his chin that very nearly made him look shy. "This sounds sappy, but that's how I thought of it. I wanted to show you that I'm not taking our love for granted. I protected it with another circle of diamonds. That's how important it is to me, do you see?"

"I do. It's so incredible that this is how you see me. That this is what you think I should wear."

Braden took the ring out of the box and, with a bit of clumsiness that Lana wanted to remember forever, placed it on the ring finger of her left hand. "Look closely."

"It's kind of hard to look at anything else."

"The outer ring isn't made up of diamonds. They're a pale blue in better light."

"Texas blue topaz?" Lana threw her arms around his neck and kissed him until he sank onto the sleeping bag, pulling her on top of him.

"The real thing," he murmured between kisses, "mined here in Hill Country." Another kiss. "This is where we met, where we fell in love, where we'll live."

"Where we'll raise a family."

Braden took her face in his hands and kept her poised over him, so that she could look him in the eye and see his concern. "We don't have to have children, Lana. You don't have to promise to be okay if you get pregnant. You only have to promise that we'll talk about every complicated thought in your head."

"Earlier tonight, when you were checking the highline, I imagined you teaching a child how to do it. The only thing wrong with that picture was the idea that we'd be single parents, exchanging custody on weekends."

"Never."

"It could have happened."

"It didn't. From today forward, it will be impossible for us to give up and go our separate ways. It's that extra circle of diamonds—I'll do anything to protect what we have."

Her breath hitched and she put her head down on his chest, turning her ear so she could hear his heart beat. She waited until the tears that had welled up subsided. Then she propped her chin on her fist, on his chest. "I don't want to cry anymore, not even happy tears. Let's do something else. Didn't you mention something about the contents of a first aid kit?"

She sat up, straddling his hips, and immediately understood that her underwear and his flannel pants were going to have to go. Soon. She reached over his head to the pile of gear, searching for the first aid kit. Her loose T-shirt dragged over his face.

"I thought it was too cold in here," he said. "I'm not supposed to touch you."

She found the first aid kit and set it on the ground above the pillow, then sat up again, wiggling a little to position herself directly over his already-firm body. "It's gotten considerably warmer, don't you think?"

She crossed her arms in front of herself, grabbed the edge of her T-shirt and pulled it over her head with a flourish. It caught for a second on the new ring she wore as she dropped it in a heap by their bedroll.

Braden sucked in a short breath, a hiss between his teeth, a sound of frustration. This time, it was exactly the type of frustration she'd wanted to cause. She gloried in her power when his body went even harder beneath her.

"We're supposed to be talking," Braden had the nerve to remind her.

"Let's see what's in this first aid kit that might be useful right about now," Lana said, and she stretched herself above him to pop open the white box, letting her bare breasts tease his mouth.

"How the hell can I talk like this?" With a growl, Braden rolled her onto her back. She shoved the waistband of his flannel pants down while he dumped out the first aid kit, grabbed a packet and tore it open with his teeth. She'd barely gotten her panties off one leg when Braden clasped her bent knee to his hip and sank deeply into her welcoming body.

Her intake of breath might have sounded like a sharp hiss in the silent Texas night, but it was only the sound of the word *yes,* and *yes* again, as Braden arched into her body, proving what a perfect match they were and had always been.

It felt familiar and new and too good. Too good—she couldn't last long if he kept moving in just that perfect motion. Excitement built rapidly. Maybe she'd last one more stroke. Two.

Three strokes, and she fell over the edge of her peak, to land, safe, in the arms of her only love.

Chapter Seventeen

Lana was late to work on Monday.

Sunday morning had begun lazily, with lovemaking in the tent. She and Braden had then dressed, rekindled the fire, set the coffeepot on its iron stand to heat and gone back into the tent and undressed again.

They'd saddled the horses and ridden a short distance before agreeing to dismount and give the horses a few moments of rest. There wasn't much else to do while the horses nibbled grass, except to conduct an experiment on the level of warmth one could maintain while having sex in the great outdoors in February's winter weather. They proved that very few clothes actually had to be removed, so staying warm was quite possible.

They broke camp, trailered the horses, rolled up the sleeping bags and packed the tent. As they drove back to the ranch house, they agreed that only desperate teenagers would resort to having sex on the uncomfortable bench seat of a work truck. There were definite benefits to being established professionals in their thirties, able to afford the most comfortable rooms in the finest hotels. Then they stopped the truck and had sex one more time, anyway.

Lana had blushed her way through a surprise dinner at Marion's house. At least, it had been a surprise to her. Braden had expected Quinn and Jamie. Lana had been the last to know she was getting engaged this weekend, apparently.

Jamie's wife, Kendry, appeared to be the most quiet and unassuming redhead Lana had ever met, until Lana walked onto the porch and caught Jamie and Kendry in an embrace that was anything but demure. Their son was a gorgeous toddler, happy and confident, and probably not destined to be an only child for long.

Braden had slept in Lana's apartment Sunday night. They'd agreed that the cardboard boxes and the mattress on the floor were more than adequate after their camping trip. They could assemble the bed properly on Monday morning, but Monday morning…well, Lana was late to work.

Myrna spotted the ring immediately, and Lana enjoyed the hugs and the camaraderie of having another woman with whom she could ooh and aah over the admittedly dazzling gems. Once she settled into her desk, Lana tried not to brood as she waited for the computer to power up. Braden was on his way to New York. She was here. But she wore his ring, and she was sure of his love, and she'd see him on Thursday night.

By Wednesday, Lana missed him so badly, she ached. Only that past Saturday, she'd been sitting by the campfire, thinking that a long-distance marriage could work. She'd been sure she could keep up her workaholic routine between passionate interludes with her fiancé. The reality was, Braden's absence was painful, and she was finding it hard to work through the pain.

Then Braden arrived on Thursday night, and Lana was happy once more, until an internal crisis in PLI required Braden to cut their long weekend short. He flew to Chicago this time, not New York.

Lana showed up to work early on Monday, then wasted her time checking weather reports for Chicago. She hoped he got out before the city was snowed in. He had to return to New York in time to finish his work there so that he'd come back to Texas on Friday.

She told herself that she could survive until Friday, but she'd forgotten how much joy there could be in physical affection. It had been years since she'd had the right to lean her head on her man's shoulder whenever she wished—in the grocery store, at the movies, in bed. Now that she'd been so vividly reminded during their shortened weekend, she wasn't sure she could live without it.

When Braden called after safely making it into New York, she closed her eyes so that she could imagine his face instead of staring at her apartment walls.

"Are you okay?" he asked. "You sound blue."

"I'm fine," she said.

The feeling of déjà vu made her slightly nauseous. They were doing it again. Living far apart, not really talking, even when they were talking. She looked at the ring on her left hand and resolved to do better this time.

Braden spoke. "I was calling to let you know—"

"Actually, honey, I am blue."

There was a short pause on the other end of the line. "What's going on?" His voice was softer. She could feel him with her.

"It's complicated."

"Tell me."

"I'm not seeing enough of you."

"That's not complicated. I feel the same way."

"The solution might be simple. I know you can't be here until Friday, but maybe I could fly up to New York tomorrow. I don't really have any vacation days accrued yet, but honestly, with this CEO's administration, no one is keeping track of that kind of thing around here."

A slightly longer pause this time. "I was calling to let you know that I'm on my way to San Francisco. It's a last-minute thing."

Her disappointment was deep. "I understand. It's fine."

He laughed, but there was no happiness in the sound. "I know that voice. Don't pretend it's fine. Help me uncomplicate it."

Lana looked at her ring. Braden was right. Clamming up and pretending everything was fine was not going to protect their relationship.

"First of all," she said, "I haven't told you today how much I love you."

"I love you, too."

"That never gets old. I've been thinking of a longer-term solution. I could quit my job and move to New York."

Braden whistled softly. "Go ahead and tell me the complicated part."

"Even if I quit my job and moved to New York for the rest of the year, there would still be Chicago and San Francisco and all those other days without you. I don't think I'd make a very good pet, waiting in a New York apartment with nothing to do except wait for my man to visit."

Braden laughed again, and this time there was a spark

of fun in the sound. "I like the idea of any man trying to turn you into a kept woman. I'm too smart to attempt it. You belong at West Central. There's something right about the former chief resident returning to chair a department. That's my family's hospital. I want the best doctors to work there, and that means you."

"I can hardly get anything done, I miss you so much."

Men's voices sounded in the background on Braden's end of the line.

"I know the feeling," he told her, his voice sounding less intimate. "I have to end this call in a minute. The plane's in line for takeoff."

Lana sighed. It looked as though there was no particular solution to this problem, but it had been good to talk honestly about her feelings.

"When we're airborne, I'll get my V.P. on the line," Braden said into the silence. "I'll have him look into leasing executive space in Austin. I could relocate now, instead of waiting for an entire facility to be completed. That doesn't eliminate trips like this one, but there are a whole lot of nights in New York I could spend in Austin instead."

"That's a wonderful idea." Lana felt like a little kid who'd just gotten a Christmas gift that her parents had told her they couldn't afford.

"I've got to go," Braden said. "I'll see you Friday."

Friday arrived, but Braden did not.

From California, he'd been called to PLI India. Urgently. No warning. He'd spent all day Friday flying not to Texas, but to the other side of the globe. Myrna had removed the pink paper hearts from their office door, because February was over.

Lana spent the weekend calculating transpacific time

zones, only calling Braden when she was sure she wouldn't wake him.

She didn't give in to her frustration. They were working on this. It might take a few more months, certainly no more than a year, and then they'd cut down a few of these separations.

His week in India became two. Myrna started decorating their office door with green paper shamrocks.

We're working on it, Lana reminded herself.

Regardless, the first weeks of their engagement had proven one thing: there was no way they could build a family like this. No matter what ring Lana wore, she'd be that single parent they'd promised each other they'd never be.

At the very least, then, she could look into some more convenient birth control while they un-complicated their current arrangement. Lana called a doctor at another hospital across town, an acquaintance that she wouldn't run into as a coworker. Lana became the patient, albeit one who was slipped into the schedule late on Friday as a professional courtesy. Before starting a new form of birth control, her new doctor ran a pregnancy test. It was a common formality, a matter of course.

Of course.

The test came back positive.

Lana was late to work on Monday. Morning sickness could do that to a person.

She'd kept herself together over the weekend. Perhaps she'd felt the panic crawl up her throat a time or two, but she'd reminded herself that history wasn't repeating itself. Braden would be with her. He'd be moving his offices to Austin soon, doing so without even knowing she was pregnant.

This pregnancy would be different. Once Braden found out she was expecting, she wouldn't have to handle everything on her own. She wouldn't be moving back to her parents' home—although she thought flying her parents to her after the baby came might be a good idea. Her mother would know what to do with a little baby. Lana certainly didn't.

The panic crawled up her throat. She pushed it back down. Again.

Everything would be fine. She'd have Braden to talk to, Braden to hold her, Braden to remind her that this baby had two parents, and it wasn't her sole responsibility to make all the correct decisions.

That was, once he got back from India. Once she had a chance to tell him she was pregnant. Lana didn't want to break the news when he was halfway around the world. She'd maintained her facade of normalcy all weekend during their phone calls. Now, despite arriving late to work, she was prepared to keep pretending nothing was different.

Myrna was already on the phones, calling pentagab patients one by one to schedule their next check-in. Lana powered up her computer and opened her daily calendar of events as if nothing had changed.

As if she weren't petrified that she might have another miscarriage.

The fear was irrational. There was no reason to expect that she'd have another early miscarriage. Then again, there was no reason not to expect it.

If it happened, then it happened, and she would deal with it. Alone. Because despite his promise that she'd never have to handle that particular misery on her own, Braden was now on another continent. India was a twenty-four-hour journey, even by private jet.

So far, this pregnancy felt just as scary and she felt just as alone as she had the last time. Being engaged to a millionaire working in India wasn't much different than being engaged to a broke grad student in Boston.

Lana skipped her morning coffee. She set a timer so that she wouldn't forget to eat lunch. She had a stilted conversation when Braden called her at eleven. His day was already over. Hers was just beginning.

She wished something at work would distract her.

On Tuesday, she got her wish. She arrived at the hospital on time, ready for work in her most businesslike dress, the navy one she'd worn the day she'd taken over the department. Television crews with their vans and tall antennae were stationed outside the lobby doors. Lana guessed that everyone who would normally be in the hospital had decided to linger outside the doors, too, waiting to see if anything would happen.

Lana stood at the edge of the crowd, but as more people arrived and piled in behind her, she started to feel penned in. She angled her body and sidestepped her way toward the door. She was going to be late to work at this rate. She needed to get to the office.

She didn't get far. An officer stopped her and the rest of the crowd from moving farther by unrolling a piece of yellow police tape. *Do Not Cross.*

Swell. Lana pulled out her cell phone from her leather bag and dialed Myrna, hoping she'd know what was happening. A major celebrity must have been admitted to the hospital. Perhaps a woman had given birth to octuplets.

Lana shook her head at that last thought. She had babies on her brain, for certain.

Just as she dialed her own office number, Lana saw the reason for the press. The lobby doors slid open, and uniformed police officers walked out, escorting the CEO of West Central. He was in handcuffs. The crowd around her shuffled excitedly, jostling for a better view. The crackers Lana had managed to keep down for breakfast threatened to come back up.

A patrol car waited only yards away, but the walk was long enough to allow the reporters to shout a barrage of questions.

"How many millions did you embezzle?"

"Do you deny the governor's charges of insurance fraud?"

"Is it true West Central is on the verge of bankruptcy?"

One policeman used his hand to make sure the CEO didn't bump his head as he got into the backseat of the patrol car.

Lana watched and listened, nauseous, while holding her phone to her ear.

"Research and Development, Myrna speaking. This call may be recorded. How can I help you?"

"It's me, Myrna. I'm outside. Have you heard the news?"

At the moment, the CEO must have decided to give the press a bigger headline. Perhaps he said something, or made some gesture, but suddenly, cameras were rushing the police car, and the crowd followed suit.

Lana was knocked to the ground, sending her phone skittering away, then pushed another foot forward on the asphalt. She barely felt the abrasions on her hands and knees, as angry as she was. Others around her had been pushed, as well. She scrambled back to her feet— no easy feat in her dress and pumps.

"Stand back," she ordered the crowd at large. It might have been like shouting in the wind, but she was right, so she did it. Two hands up, she repeated her order, stepping slightly to her left so that she was blocking the crowd from walking on another downed woman, a person several decades her senior.

The initial surge stalled of its own accord, and Lana turned immediately to link an arm with the large woman, who was floundering about ineffectively. "Come on, pull on me. Let's get you up."

No sooner had she gotten the woman on her feet again than the crowd surged for a second time. The woman went down again with a shriek. Their arms linked, she hauled Lana down with her, so that Lana landed on her back on top of her. Instinctively, she turned to roll off the woman, putting her already-raw hand down on the asphalt. It hurt the second time, really hurt, and then someone kicked her in the back, in the kidney.

No! I'm pregnant! The words roared through her mind, but she didn't make a sound. On her knees, she hunched over, arms crossed over herself protectively, until Kendry MacDowell called her name, an eternity of minutes later.

Lana held her cafeteria spoon gingerly. The heels of her palms protested if she forgot about the morning's chaos and grabbed something normally. She ate her yogurt and kicked back in Montgomery's chair as she examined Kendry's expertly applied gauze patches on her palms and knees.

They were almost amusing. The last time she'd had these exact same injuries, she'd been a child who'd fallen while roller-skating on a sidewalk. Then the best mother in the world had patched her up. This time, Kendry had done it with equal dexterity. Kendry was also a great mother, and she worked in the hospital's day-care center, to boot.

It looked as though Lana was still on track to get a

shot at mothering herself. She'd stopped in the ladies'
room at least a half dozen times since this morning, but
there was no bleeding. Her back might bruise where
she'd been kicked, but she was still pregnant.

Thus, she was eating this yogurt instead of skipping
lunch, even if it stung her hands to do so. It was almost
three in the afternoon, but finally, she'd given up on
her conference call with a biotech firm and gone to get
some food for herself. No one in the industry was willing to make West Central their research site right now,
not after this morning's debacle with the CEO. Who
would begin a study with a hospital that might go bankrupt in a few days?

West Central could cease to exist. It didn't seem possible. She'd practically lived here as a resident. She'd
fallen in love here, been proposed to here and even miscarried here when she was chief resident. The hospital
had served Austin for decades, after Braden's father had
worked so hard to get it started.

Poor Braden. His father's portrait hung in the lobby.
She'd seen him look at it a hundred times during their
residency. His father's legacy could disappear, ground
into financial ruin by an unscrupulous CEO who had
been imported from another hospital system in another
state by an apathetic board.

Lana flipped her injured hand over and looked at her
engagement ring. She and Braden had promised to protect what was important. West Central was important,
but its protectors had done a lousy job.

Until now. Quinn had taken a vacancy on the board
recently. They were meeting at this moment, and she
doubted Quinn was being a docile junior board member.
Kendry had told Lana this morning that Jamie was going
to take over as chair of the emergency department this

spring. And she, Lana Donnoli, was chairing research and development. She would change her last name to MacDowell this year. Could the new influx of MacDowells protect West Central, or was it all too little, too late?

Her phone rang. She grabbed it without thinking and felt the sting of her abraded palm.

"Ow. Hello?"

"Why didn't you call me?" Braden's anger was palpable, undiminished by time and space as it pinged from India to a satellite to her ear.

She did the math. "It's two in the morning for you. You should be sleeping."

"I just saw the news. On my phone. For God's sake, what did you think I'd do when I saw that *on my phone?*"

"I know it's hard because it was your dad's hospital, but it's not over. No one knows exactly how much money is missing. Now that the CEO is in custody, maybe they'll find some of it. West Central hasn't gone under yet."

Braden sounded even more angry. "Do you think I give a damn about some white-collar criminal? I'm talking about you. How badly are you hurt?"

"You know about that?"

"I saw the photo. That was you, in the navy dress. You're supposed to call me when you need me, damn it. Call me."

"I don't know what photo you're talking about." Within moments, her internet search turned up scenes of the CEO's apprehension. "These pictures are all very… Oh. I see it now."

There she was, landing on her hand when she'd been pushed down the second time. She looked as though she was in midair, but she'd been rolling off the woman who'd dragged her down. It was a pretty spectacular action shot, probably a still from one of the TV cameras. Braden must have thought the worst.

"Honey, it wasn't that bad."

Except for the part where I got kicked and I was scared it would cause a miscarriage and Kendry had to calm me down and I had to swear her to secrecy after freaking out and throwing up my crackers. That part was bad.

"What did Jamie say?" Braden demanded.

"I didn't go to see him. I just skinned my knees and my hands a bit." She tried to keep it light, knowing Braden's short, impatient tone came from worry.

"Damn it, Lana. From now on, when I'm not there, you go see Jamie. Period."

The *period* almost made her lose her temper. She didn't need to be given orders. "Don't you think it's overkill to have the head of emergency look at some skinned knees?"

"No. You see Jamie, and then you call me."

"You're in India. Why would I call when there is nothing you can do?"

"Because I'm your fiancé." He practically roared the words at her.

She understood, to a point, but it was time they got a few things straight. "You're my fiancé, and you love me. I know that, Braden, I really do. But if I'd called to tell you that West Central might go bankrupt and I got trampled, what could you have done about it? Nothing, because you're not here. I love you, too, you know. I'm not going to call and dump problems on your shoulders that will weigh you down. If you are in town, and I think you can help, I'll let you know."

"Otherwise, I'm not part of your life."

"Otherwise, you'll have to trust me to handle things by myself when you aren't here. This is our reality."

And that, she realized, was the bottom line. There was no escaping reality. They loved one another, but they were going to be apart very often. She'd have to deal with it, because there would be no other man for her, ever. Braden was her one and only.

"I'm a pretty capable person, Braden. We'll get used to it."

"When you're trampled by a mob, I want to know."

"Fair enough. But I wouldn't say this was a mob. It was more of a small crowd."

Silence.

Lana waited, but Braden didn't play their game. Maybe he was tired; it was two in the morning in his part of the world. "That was a joke, honey. Is it small, or is it a crowd? You can't have both."

"No, you can't. Sometimes you have to choose."

The next morning, a few TV cameras were still stationed outside the hospital's main doors. Lana decided to enter through the emergency room, feeling a little silly for being so cautious. Jamie kissed her cheek when she passed him, making her smile. She would always miss Braden when he was out of town, but Jamie reminded her that she would always have family here.

She channeled her new attitude into a productive morning. She was going to be married to Braden, she was going to have a baby, and she was going to do her part to help West Central. Ergo, she cruised a few wedding websites, she contacted a woman who'd been in her residency program who was also pregnant, and she solidified West Central's current studies with each of their respective sponsors.

She even remembered when it was time to eat lunch.

"I'm going out for lunch," Myrna announced, standing up and gathering her purse. "Can I bring you anything, Dr. Donnoli?"

"No, I'm all set." She'd packed a healthy brown-bag lunch. By working through lunch, she'd be able to leave on time for once. She'd go home, eat a decent dinner and put her feet up. Braden usually called her around eight, and she planned to take his call from the comfort of her sofa. It was a baby step for a workaholic, but she felt as if it was a step in the right direction.

Myrna shut the door as she left. Moments later, she rushed back in.

Lana looked up from her three-ring binder. "Did you forget something?"

"Flowers!"

Myrna triumphantly placed a planter on Lana's desk.

"Texas bluebonnets," Lana whispered. They were securely blooming in rich soil, ready to be transplanted in better weather. She hadn't known anyone could buy blooming bluebonnets in March.

"Let me find out the meaning of bluebonnets for you," Myrna said.

"I know what these mean." She didn't need to look at the card. The bluebonnets, the symbol of Texas, could only have been a gift from Braden. They meant he missed her. He wanted to be in Texas, with her. Lana felt teary, but she didn't blame hormones. It was just plain old love.

"If you already know about the flowers, then I'll be going. You have a nice lunch hour."

"Thank you, Myrna."

A deep, masculine voice echoed hers. "Thank you, Myrna."

"Braden," Lana gasped. Then she was out of her chair, flying across the room to tackle him as he was closing her office door. She murmured his name between kisses of disbelief, over and over, until their kisses lengthened, deepened, and once more, words were senseless. This was Braden. This was her heart, her other half, her love.

"Lock the door," she said, reaching for his belt buckle. He was in a business suit. She hadn't tried to undo this type of sleek belt before, and she wasn't taking any chances. She used two hands.

"Lana."

"I'm finally going to appreciate that ridiculously over-sized desk chair."

"Darlin', I'm fixing to address the board again in a few minutes. What are you doing later tonight?"

"Ooh, the Texas drawl is back. You really know how to make a girl melt." She let go of his belt, but she still slid both arms around his waist and held him close.

He grinned, but he shook the cuff of his suit jacket back to check his watch. As she'd been doing for the past two weeks, Lana automatically thought about time zones and travel.

She did the math. "How did you get here so fast? We were just talking yesterday at three. It's barely noon."

Braden kissed each corner of her mouth, then began tucking her hair behind her ear. He looked very serious. "I ordered that plane toward home within two seconds of seeing that photo."

"Oh, Braden." It was a little overwhelming, to be the center of his world once more.

"I was already in the air when I called you. It took a while for me to get past the fact that you were being hurt to read the headline that went with the photo."

"I've got some inside info on why the CEO was arrested. Do you remember that Dr. Montgomery's laptop had turned up missing?"

"Did it turn up, or was it missing? It can't be both."

"Very funny. It was missing. Montgomery had taken it with him, because he'd stored all his evidence against the CEO in it. He blew the whistle. That laptop has turned up at the FBI."

"I always liked Montgomery."

"Me, too. I'm still not happy that he left this department in debt, but he was trying to help your mom with those studies, and he did something about that CEO when the board wouldn't, so I can't be mad at him. Much."

She let go of Braden's waist only to grab his lapels and pull him closer. "Since you traveled halfway around the world to check on me and my skinned knees, maybe we should..." Braden's earlier words clicked into place. "Wait a minute."

"Maybe we should wait a minute?"

"Did you say you have to address the board? *Again?* Could you explain that, please?"

"On the plane, after I hung up with you, I started calling the members of the board, one by one. They were waiting for me when I landed. We talked. They're taking a vote right now, but it's only a formality."

"They're voting on what?" Lana was jumping to conclusions with lightning speed, but she wanted to hear Braden say it to make it all real.

Braden kissed her again. "Sometimes the solution to a complicated situation is simple. I want to live with you seven days a week, three hundred sixty-five days a year. I need to be here. West Central needs a new CEO. It's very simple."

"There's not going to be anything simple about taking over as CEO. As someone once said to me, you're

starting out in a hole you didn't dig. A very big hole."
Still holding his lapels, she gave him a gentle shake. "I'm
worried about you. This is a huge task."

He raised his brow. "I'm very good at un-complicating
things. Calculated risks are my specialty. I've run some
preliminary numbers. I think West Central can make it."

She reached up to smooth his brow. "Well, then, good
luck with your patient, Dr. MacDowell. If anyone can
save West Central, you can. You are terribly overquali-
fied, and I hope the board realizes it."

"The compensation package has some priceless benefits. I'll be your boss. If I tell you to call me, you're
going to have to call me."

It was just the opening Lana needed. She struggled to
maintain a straight face as she smoothed the lapels she'd
been holding and took a step back. "I may need to turn
in my notice, boss. I've been thinking about your comment that I'm not practicing medicine. Do you remember Marcy Lewiston, from our residency? She's with a
practice here in town. She's expecting a baby, and she
wants to cut her hours back. I'd be job-sharing with her,
seeing patients two days a week."

Braden scooped her up in a bear hug. "I think that's
terrific. You were meant to be in patient care, not stuck
behind a desk."

She couldn't keep a straight face any longer as he put
her back on her feet. "Marcy isn't due until the fall, so
I've got some time to get this department pointed in the
right direction. I have to say that, all in all, it sounds—"
she paused and winked "—awfully good."

He jumped on her oxymoron immediately. "It can't be
awfully good. It has to be awful, or it has to be good."

Lana laughed, a bubble of happiness that couldn't
be contained. "It's like saying I'm a little bit pregnant."

"No one is a little bit pregnant. You're either pregnant or…you're…"

Snug in his arms, she felt the small jolt when her meaning hit him.

"…not. Lana. Are you pregnant?"

She held up her thumb and forefinger an inch apart. "Just a little bit. Maybe four weeks or so?"

Braden pulled her with him as he collapsed against the office door. They kissed, surrounded by shamrocks, until a green paper clover came loose and fluttered down to catch in Lana's hair.

"I think that means you are going to get very lucky after your board meeting," Lana said.

Braden slowly drew the shamrock out of her hair. "I'm already the luckiest man in Texas. As long as I have you, I don't need any other good-luck charms."

* * * * *

A sneaky peek at next month...

Cherish™

ROMANCE TO MELT THE HEART EVERY TIME

My wish list for next month's titles...

In stores from 21st February 2014:

❏ The Returning Hero – Soraya Lane

& Road Trip With the Eligible Bachelor – Michelle Douglas

❏ Lassoed by Fortune – Marie Ferrarella

& Celebration's Family – Nancy Robards Thompson

In stores from 7th March 2014:

❏ Safe in the Tycoon's Arms – Jennifer Faye

& The Secrets of Her Past – Emilie Rose

❏ Awakened By His Touch – Nikki Logan

& Finding Family...and Forever? – Teresa Southwick

Available at WHSmith, Tesco, Asda, Eason, Amazon and Apple

Just can't wait?

Visit us Online

You can buy our books online a month before they hit the shops! **www.millsandboon.co.uk**

0214/23

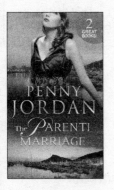

MILLS & BOON
Book Club

Join the Mills & Boon Book Club

Want to read more **Cherish**™ books?
We're offering you **2 more** absolutely **FREE!**

We'll also treat you to these fabulous extras:

- Exclusive offers and much more!

- FREE home delivery

- FREE books and gifts with our special rewards scheme

Get your free books now!

visit www.millsandboon.co.uk/bookclub
or call Customer Relations on 020 8288 2888

Discover more romance at

www.millsandboon.co.uk